T L

Jeremy had known something was going to happen. He had known it from the moment they had arrived in New York – and he had seen it in some sort of vision. The power, telepathy or whatever you liked to call it, had behaved in a way that was completely new and that scared Nicholas. He remembered the look on his brother's face. Jeremy had been terrified, on the edge of madness. What had he seen? Whatever it was, it had taken him . . .

Also by Anthony Horowitz
in Magnet Books

The Devil's Door-Bell
The Night of the Scorpion

ANTHONY HOROWITZ

THE SILVER CITADEL

A Magnet Book

First published 1987 by Methuen Children's Books Ltd
This Magnet edition published 1987 by
Methuen Children's Books Ltd
11 New Fetter Lane, London EC4P 4EE

Printed in Great Britain by
Richard Clay Ltd, Bungay, Suffolk

ISBN 0 416 02572 2

= CONTENTS =

= ONE =

Off Broadway

THE BLACK LIMOUSINE drove slowly down the narrow street, its engine so quiet that it seemed to be propelled by some mysterious power. Its windows were made of smoked glass, too dark to see through from outside. The street was so narrow, the car's wheels almost touched the sidewalk on both sides. One wheel rode over an empty Coca-Cola can, crushing it, then spun the twisted metal aside. The car stopped. Two men got out.

"Is this the place, Worm?" the older man asked.

"Yes, Mr. Banes," Worm replied. "This is it."

The Comedy Theatre was on the edge of Manhattan, in an area called Greenwich Village. It was about as far from the bright lights of Broadway as a New York theater can get. Another few blocks and it would have tumbled into the dark waters of the Hudson River. Nobody would have missed it.

It looked more like a dilapidated restaurant than a theater. Above the front door the two words "Comedy Theatre" had once hung in brilliant green neon lights, but over the years the letters had broken one at a time until it was the advertisement "Come . . . eat . . ." that flashed from noon to night. A smell of burning oil lingered around the building and a line of trash cans overflowing with rotten food lined the curb in front of it.

It was a small, crooked building, slumped between a fenced-off parking lot and a Laundromat. There was a white pillar on each side of the entrance, but these had crumbled away like mouldy sticks of rock. Dust clung to the windows. Sneeze and you'd think the whole place would collapse.

The man called Mr. Banes walked forward and stood in front of a wooden bulletin board outside the theater. A sheet of paper had been pinned there, one corner flapping in the breeze, the hand-colored letters already fading in the warm October sunlight. It read:

DON WHITE
presents
OUT OF THIS WORLD

An evening's journey
into the land beyond
the boundaries of science

Telepathy
Hypnotism
ESP
Clairvoyance
Spiritualism

Featuring
Jeremy and Nicholas Helsey,
the talk of seventeen cities

"Jeremy and Nicholas Helsey," Mr. Banes muttered to himself.

"That's the ones, Mr. Banes," Worm said, coming up behind him. "They're the ones I told you about."

"I know they are," Mr. Banes snarled.

"Of course, Mr. Banes. Of course you do. I didn't mean—" Worm bit his thumb nervously.

"We'll go in."

"If you say so, Mr. Banes. Of course. If you say it, we'll do it."

Five hundred yards away from the bulletin board, on the other side of a busy street, a wooden jetty pointed out into the Hudson River. Two boys were standing at the end of it, watching the sun set behind the distant Statue of Liberty. The sky was a powdery blue, streaked with orange and pink.

Against this glowing backdrop, helicopters buzzed like metallic flies over the sluggish waters. To the left, the two monoliths of the World Trade Center stuck out like cutouts in a pop-up book.

The boys were twins. Both had straw-colored hair falling in an untidy fringe over their brown eyes. Both had thin faces and prominent cheekbones. But for the fact that one was wearing a parka and jeans while the other wore a baggy red sweater and grey cords, they could have been mirror images.

The boy in the sweater was the first to speak. "I don't like this city," he said.

"We haven't seen it yet, Jem," his brother replied.

Jeremy dug into his pants pocket and pulled out a packet of chewing gum. He unwrapped a piece with a quick, nervous movement, rolled it up, and put it into his mouth.

"New York," he muttered.

"What's wrong with it, Jem?"

"I don't know." He brushed the hair out of his eyes. "There's something. I can feel it."

Nicholas stood silently, trying to clamp down the worry he felt. His brother had been born only five minutes before him, but sometimes he seemed five years older. The two of them were barely fourteen. He shivered. There was a slight chill in the air, but it was vague, distant, no more than a whisper of the winter to come.

"It can't be worse than Boston," he said.

They had been touring now for six months. Philadelphia, Atlanta, Boston . . . they had soon lost track of the cities. Half-empty theater had followed half-empty theater, crummy hotel after crummy hotel. On a good night they might attract an audience of a hundred people or more. But there were few good nights. It was getting harder to find theaters that would book them at all. As theater managers said, the paranormal was old hat. Just conjuring without the rabbit.

Not that either of them had ever wanted a career in the theater. It had been forced on them, like everything else in their lives. Once, a long time ago, things had been different. Standing, watching his brother chew the gum, Nicholas tried to remember the times before the accident, before Uncle Don.

Their parents were Americans living in England and the boys were brought up there. Their father worked for a travel company, managing the London office. Their mother sold paintings in a small art gallery. Theirs had been a happy, disorganized household. People were always dropping in. Meals were never on time. Nobody ever planned anything. And then, when the twins were just ten years old, six years after they had arrived in England, Mr. and Mrs. Helsey were killed in a car crash.

The weeks that followed had been a nightmare—friends who wanted to help but who could do nothing, transatlantic letters and telephone calls, strangers coming in and out of the house, talking in low voices and avoiding Jeremy and Nicholas as though they were afraid of them. There had been only one relative willing to take the boys—provided the generous sum from the Helseys' insurance policy came with them. To Jeremy and Nicholas he was just a name on a sheet of paper—Don White, used car salesman, Chicago. Their parents had never spoken of him. They had never seen a photograph of him. And now they were his.

He had shipped the two brothers back to America as if they had been suitcases that had gone astray. He had poured the money into his flagging business, and when that had finally gone bust, into cheap whiskey that he had poured into himself. They spent three years in Chicago, living in a rundown apartment, going to a school where the other children smoked, drank, and fought. Usually, their Uncle Don ignored them. Only when he was very drunk was he cruel to them. That was before he discovered their power.

Jeremy and Nicholas had always been close, not just in the ordinary way brothers are, but in that peculiar way known to many twins. When Jeremy fell ill with whooping cough, so had Nicholas. On the day that Nicholas burned his hand on a hot pan, a mysterious swelling had appeared in exactly the same place on Jeremy's hand. Somehow, one always knew where the other was without being told. More than that, each could tell how the other was feeling: sad, happy, hungry, thirsty . . . whatever. It was as if they spent part of their lives inside each other's minds.

And as they had grown older, their affinity had become stranger, more unpredictable. They had almost been expelled from one school when they had submitted identical answers to an examination, with identical mistakes. Once Nicholas had been attacked by a gang of bullies and Jeremy had come running to help him from a block away, even though Nicholas had never opened his mouth to cry for help. They were twelve at the time, and it was then that they knew. Neither of them said anything. Somehow—perhaps it was the stillness in the air—they knew something was going to happen.

"You can hear me, can't you, Nick."

"Yes, Jem. I can hear you."

They hadn't spoken the words. They had thought them.

Across the street, Don White had watched them from the window of his apartment and his eyes had narrowed, his own thoughts racing ahead of them.

Now Nicholas could sense his brother's mood as keenly as if it were his own. And he was worried. Jeremy had always been the stronger of the two, always the one to come running when he was in trouble. When Uncle Don was drunk and mean, Jeremy would be there, putting himself firmly between the two of them. Jeremy was several pounds heavier than his brother, although it didn't show. Nicholas had always looked on him as an older brother, sometimes even as a replacement for their father.

Inevitably, Jeremy had suffered more in the four years they had spent with Don White. But he was coming to the end of his tether. His short, edgy movements were just one danger signal, one crack in the facade. Jeremy needed help. And Nicholas wondered if he had the strength to give it.

"It's time to go in," Jeremy said. "We ought to change for the show."

"I wish we didn't have to do it." Nicholas pushed his hands into his pockets and kicked at an empty cigarette pack.

Jeremy gave him a half smile. "Only four more years and we'll be independent, Nick," he said. "We'll be able to go our own way."

"But will we last that long?"

"We've got to."

Don White glanced at the two men sitting opposite his desk and decided that he definitely didn't like them.

The younger of the two, the one called Worm, was in his late twenties, dressed in black leather pants and a white T-shirt stretched tight over a muscular body. Yet all the muscles were somehow in the wrong places. It was as if he had been working out at a hopelessly inept gymnasium. How else do you develop biceps in your neck? His hair was long and blond, hanging down in damp strands. He had a face like a paper bag that somebody had just blown up.

There could have been no more peculiar companion for Mr. Banes. The older man was tall and thin, quite bald, with perfectly round wire-framed glasses. His skin was the color of granite, scarred by a shadowy mustache that looked like so many cigarette burns across his upper lip. He wore the largest hearing aid Don White had ever seen. It was connected to the man's left ear by a thick wire that threatened to tear the whole thing from his head. Even the volume control was the size of a coat button. Despite the weather, Mr. Banes was dressed in a very dark, old-fashioned three-piece suit. He was about forty years old, and yet if he had died and been buried forty years before, he would have looked much the same. Mr. Banes wasn't quite alive.

Don White definitely didn't like the two men sitting opposite him. But so long as they were worth money to him, he was prepared to put up with them.

"The kids were eleven when I realized what they'd got," he was saying. "Their power, I mean. There was always something creepy about them, the way they hung around together. If I belted one of them"—he rubbed the heavy signet ring on his hand—"it was like the other felt it too. When my business went down the tube, I was gonna just dump them. But then I had this idea . . . ."

He sucked at his cigar. Already the leaves were sodden and mushy, the tobacco staining his teeth brown.

"I figured I'd put them on the stage. I mean, I'd looked after those kids. If it wasn't for me, they'd have been stuck in some dump in England. An orphanage or something. If it wasn't for their Uncle Don, they'd have been nowhere."

Don White jammed the cigar back into his mouth and waited for the two men to speak. He was a short man, but powerfully built. At one stage in his career he had been a professional wrestler—until the day when he had been disqualified for biting off his opponent's ear. He sensed the two men were trying to frighten him, but he wasn't afraid of anyone. He smiled at them defiantly through a cloud of smoke.

Mr. Banes spoke for the first time.

"Ten thousand dollars," he said.

"Each," Don White replied.

"For the two of them."

"Now, wait a minute!" Don White flicked ash in the direction of the wastebasket. It missed and disintegrated on the carpet. "I don't know what you want the kids for. That's your business. But they're worth more than five thousand dollars each. I mean, they can read each other's minds, for God's sake!"

"So you say, Mr. White."

Don White crushed the cigar out in a tin ashtray. "You'll believe me when you see them. Honest! Is there no trust left in the world?" He picked a piece of tobacco leaf out from between his teeth. "All right. I admit it," he continued. "The rest of the show is all phony. I couldn't put the kids on the stage by themselves. So I advertised. I picked up a bunch of fakes and has-beens. So okay. My hypnotist couldn't hypnotize a lettuce. The clairvoyant can't even remember the past, let alone see into the future. But they're just the window dressing. The boys are different. They can read minds like you and I can read books. They're dynamite!"

"Then why are you so eager to be rid of them?"

"Because I can use the money more than I can use them. Look at this dump! Nobody will pay to see the paranormal anymore. They don't believe in it. It's like the guy who used to bend spoons. One day he's front-page news. The next he's forgotten. That's why I brought the kids to New York. I met a guy in a bar in Boston. He told me there were people interested in kids with powers. I don't know why and I don't want to know. But they've got power. You see for yourself."

Mr. Banes turned to his partner.

"What do you think, Worm?"

"I agree with you, Mr. Banes."

"You always do, Worm." Mr. Banes adjusted his hearing aid with a skeletal finger. "Very well, Mr. White. We'll watch the performance tonight. If I think they have what we're looking for, we'll take them immediately afterward. You will be paid fifteen thousand dollars for the two of them." He held up his hand to forestall any argument.

"That's my last offer. You can take the money and leave New York.

"But if I find you've been wasting my time"—he smiled coldly, the cigarette-burn mustache writhing—"then it is you who will pay."

= TWO =

The Wall

THEY HAD SOLD sixty-two tickets for the show that night. There were sixty-four people in the audience.

Mr. Banes and his companion were sitting at the very back, as far into the shadows as they could get. They had not come alone. Outside the Comedy Theatre there was a white van parked in the street, a third man leaning against the door, smoking a cigarette, and a fourth behind the wheel. Two more men stood near the entrance to the theater, their eyes darting left and right along the street. One of them carried a radio receiver, waiting for a signal.

It was nine o'clock. Inside the theater, the hypnotist was just finishing his act. He was an elderly man with straggling gray hair and bulging eyes. He was holding a pin. A volunteer from the audience sat in a chair opposite him.

"You are completely in my power," the hypnotist was saying. "You can feel nothing in your left leg . . . nothing at all."

He leaned forward and jabbed the pin into the volunteer's leg. The volunteer yelled. Everyone in the audience laughed—everyone except for Mr. Banes, who showed only a flicker of irritation.

The hypnotist made a hasty bow and left the stage while the volunteer limped back to his seat. Then, as the curtain swept shut behind him, Don White appeared, dressed in a moth-eaten gold lamé jacket and carrying a microphone.

"That was the Great Grandini," he said. "And now, ladies

and gentlemen, the climax of our journey into the unknown. They've amazed and astounded audiences in no fewer than seventeen cities. Now they're here in New York for the first and perhaps"—he smiled to himself—"the last time. Ladies and gentlemen, I am proud to present the telepathic twins . . . Jeremy and Nicholas Helsey."

There was a smattering of applause. Mr. Banes and Worm drew themselves up, their eyes narrowing. The curtain drew back to reveal Jeremy and Nicholas standing alone on the stage. They had changed into uniform black trousers and black shirts, open at the neck. Jeremy was holding a book of quotations. Nicholas held a blindfold and a black cotton bag. There was a plain wooden chair on the stage behind him.

"Good evening. My name is Jeremy Helsey. My brother and I are about to give a demonstration of the power of telepathy—or mind reading." Jeremy spoke the words automatically, without emotion. "First, let me assure you that there is no trickery involved. What you are about to see is real. Now I would like some members of the audience to examine the blindfold and the bag to confirm that it is impossible to see through them."

While Jeremy spoke, Nicholas handed the two props into the front row. The bag and the blindfold were passed along, the audience holding the dark material up to their eyes. Already the boys had made an impact on them. It was easy to see the youths hated what they were doing.

Meanwhile, Jeremy had moved farther into the auditorium. He went about halfway down the aisle and stood beside a middle-aged man who had come to the show with his wife.

"Excuse me, sir," Jeremy said. "Have we ever met?"

"No." The man shook his head. His wife giggled.

"Then would you please take this book of quotations. You will note that it has over four hundred pages. Please open it anywhere, choose a quotation, and pass it back to me."

The man did as he was told. Jeremy took the book and read the quotation that the man had chosen, concentrating on every word. He had done it many times before, but it was still difficult to explain what he did. It was as if he were trying to memorize the words, channeling them into some secret compartment in his mind. Except that he could forget them instantly. Once they had reached that compartment, he could *transmit* them. There was no other word to describe it. He could actually feel them traveling out of him.

"Nicholas?" Jeremy called out.

" *'Good things of day begin to droop and drowse; While night's black agents to their preys do rouse.'* " Nicholas quoted it exactly. "It's from Shakespeare's *Macbeth*," he added.

Jeremy handed the book back to the man. "Is that correct?" he asked.

"Yes," the man stammered.

"And is that the quotation you chose?"

"Yes . . . yes, it is!"

Jeremy took the book and closed it. There was loud applause for the first time that evening as the audience examined the two boys more closely. Of course it was a trick. It had to be a trick. But how on earth was it done?

Watching from the wings, Don White smiled to himself, dreaming of fifteen thousand dollars. In the back row Mr. Banes smiled too.

"They have it," he whispered. "Give the signal, Worm. . . ."

Worm pulled out a radio and held it close to his lips. "Amber," he said.

And outside the theater one of the men threw down his cigarette and stubbed it out with his heel.

"We're going in," he said.

Nicholas was standing on the stage, waiting. Jeremy went back and stood next to his brother. "The blindfold and the bag have been examined," he said. "My brother will now make it impossible for me to see anything."

Carefully Nicholas tied the blindfold around Jeremy's eyes and then pulled the bag right over his head. It came down as far as his neck. Dressed in black, he looked like a prisoner about to be hanged. Finally Nicholas led him to the chair and sat him down with his back facing the audience. Now it was his turn to take over the presentation.

"I have here a pack of cards," he said as once again he walked into the audience. He stopped in front of another man. "Could you please choose one and show it to me?" He held a fan of cards in front of the man. The man chose one.

"The queen of spades," Jeremy said, his voice muffled beneath the mask.

The man held up the queen of spades. The audience applauded for a second time, even more loudly than before. Putting the cards away, Nicholas moved forward a few more rows. This time he stopped beside a young woman.

"What I would like now is for someone to give me an object . . . any object." He turned to the woman. "You, please, madam. Give me anything out of your handbag."

The woman opened her handbag and took something out. She placed it in his hand.

"It's a key," Jeremy said from the stage.

Nicholas held up the key before giving it back to the woman. Then, to renewed applause, he continued up the aisle to the back of the theater. "For my third experiment, I need a business card or a driver's license," he said. "Anything with a name and address on it." He stopped and turned to the nearest person. "Could I have something from you, sir?"

Usually Nicholas didn't take much notice of the people in the audience. He would use them for an effect and then forget them. But he couldn't help noticing the man he had just approached, the horrible, twisted muscles under the T-shirt, the damp strands of yellow hair. The man had flinched away from him, as though he didn't want to be touched. Now he turned to his companion, and Nicholas glimpsed the curve of a hearing aid as the companion nodded.

The man took out his wallet and produced a plastic-covered security card. There was a bad photograph of himself glued to one side. His eyes had caught the flash from the camera and shone, a congealed yellow. Next to the photograph was a name. Nicholas read it: Albert Worm, The Citadel, New York. The card gave neither the man's occupation nor his telephone number. As Nicholas took it, their hands brushed and he shivered. It was like touching a corpse.

On the stage Jeremy shivered too. His hand had gone numb. He tried to concentrate on the name that his brother was sending him, but he could not gather his thoughts. The chill was in his bones, throbbing through his arm. It reached his shoulder, then stretched out to wind itself around his neck.

Suddenly the darkness seemed to become solid, as solid as the mask that pressed against his face, suffocating him. Jeremy tried to cry out, but he could barely breathe. He was trapped in an immense darkness and he could feel the panic welling up inside him, clawing at him like a caged animal.

"Jeremy . . ."

The voice was not his brother's. It was a hard, cruel voice that belonged to neither man nor woman. Then it was as if a door had opened at the end of the long corridor of his consciousness. He found himself hurtling toward it, unable to stop, his feet not even touching the ground. Unwillingly he looked out into the light. Now he could see the street outside the theater. There was a van waiting, its back open. Men were running toward the theater, guns in their hands.

The scene shimmered and changed. Now he could see Nicholas, perched on a wall, his hands reaching down. His brother's face was filled with despair, his eyes wide, blood trickling from a wound under his hair. He heard footsteps running toward him but could not turn around. His brother was shouting at him, but he could hear nothing. He reached out for the hand. It was too far away. Stretching every muscle, he reached again. Now he brushed his brother's fingertips. The steps were getting closer. He made one last effort, jumped, and grabbed at empty air.

"Jeremy . . ."

That dreadful, mocking voice whispered again and grey clouds rolled over the vision only to separate again a moment later. There was something in front of him, a face. Slowly it came into focus. There were two eyes staring into his own. Who was it? The face twisted. Then, at last, he could see. He could see . . .

He screamed.

Inside the theater Nicholas spun around. The audience broke into an excited murmur. He had been waiting for Jeremy to speak, to read out the name on the card. But Jeremy had stood up, knocking over the chair. He was staggering on the stage like a madman, tearing at the mask with helpless fingers. Dropping the pass, Nicholas ran back, climbed the steps, and reached him. With one quick movement he tore off the hood, then pulled away the blindfold. But still his brother didn't see him. His face was bathed in sweat, his eyes far away.

"Jeremy!" he shouted, shaking him. "Jeremy!"

His brother whimpered, unable to speak. It was a sound that made Nicholas feel sick inside.

"Jeremy! What is it? What happened?"

"Nick . . . help me . . ."

Forgetting the audience, Nicholas put his arm around his brother and helped him from the stage. At the back of the theater Mr. Banes seized the radio transmitter from Worm and spoke rapidly into it.

"Condition green. Do you read me? Green!"

Outside, the waiting men moved to surround the theater while the van's engine coughed and sprang to life.

"Ladies and gentlemen, please don't be alarmed. The boys are tired. It's nothing to worry about. . . ."

While Don White took over onstage, Nicholas half-carried his brother into the tiny office that passed as a dressing room. Their street clothes hung on a rack against one wall. A chipped mirror surrounded by light bulbs hung on another. Only two of the light bulbs were working.

Jeremy sat down heavily. Some of the blood had returned to his face, but he was still breathing unevenly.

"What happened, Jeremy?" Nicholas asked.

"I don't know." Jeremy took a deep breath. "Listen, Nicholas. We've got to get out of here."

"Out of here? Where? Why?"

"I don't know!" Jeremy shouted the words. Then he pulled himself together, pressing his fingers to his temples. "I'm sorry, Nick. I'm sorry. We've just got to go. We're in danger. There are people . . ."

"What people?" But Nicholas remembered touching the man in the audience, and suddenly he was afraid.

"I don't know, Nick. I don't know anything. I tell you . . . there's something wrong in this place . . . New York. We've got to move."

"But where will we go?"

"It doesn't matter. Just away."

"Hadn't we better change?"

"There isn't time."

Even so, Nicholas pulled on his parka. His mind was in a whirl. It had all happened so quickly. What had happened? He still had no idea.

Jeremy reached the door. Then he paused and turned round.

"Listen, Nick," he said. "I don't know what's going to happen to us. But there's something. I know this is going to sound stupid . . . but whatever happens . . . I'm your brother, Nick. I always will be."

Then he opened the door.

It was quiet outside. Don White had brought back the clairvoyant for an encore and Nicholas could hear her voice, summoning up somebody's dead grandmother. They stepped into the empty corridor and began to move toward the back exit, the unshaded lights casting huge shadows ahead of them. They had taken only ten paces when they heard the sound of someone approaching. It was too late to turn back. Jeremy reached for the nearest door, opened it, and hurried into the room, pulling Nicholas behind him.

The Great Grandini gazed at them in astonishment. He was sitting in his shabby suit, holding a bottle of cheap wine. The boys hardly knew him. They seldom if ever spoke to any of the other performers. Now Jeremy raised a finger to his lips to silence him, his eyes darting around the room. There was a folding screen in one corner. Gesturing to Nicholas, he stepped behind it. The two of them had only just concealed themselves when the door opened.

"Excuse me," a voice said. It was coldly polite. "We're looking for the two Helsey boys. Have you seen them?"

There was a long silence. Nicholas froze. The hypnotist owed them no favors. Would he give them away?

Then he spoke. "No," he said. "Have you tried their dressing room?"

"Where is it?"

"Four doors down on the right. And next time try knocking."

The door slammed shut.

Jeremy and Nicholas came out from their hiding place. The hypnotist looked at them, a worried expression on his face.

"Are you kids in trouble?" he asked.

"Yes," Jeremy said.

"What have you done?"

"We haven't done anything."

"Well, I'd look out. Those were pretty mean-looking people."

The two boys went over to the door and opened it softly.

"Thanks a lot," Nicholas said.

"Good luck, kid." The Great Grandini raised the wine bottle.

There was nobody outside. Treading carefully now, trying not to make any noise, they hurried down the corridor. There was a fire exit at the far end, but it could have been a mile away. Nicholas felt as if he were in a nightmare. The faster he went, the farther away the door seemed to be. Then a voice called out behind them.

"You! Stop!"

The two boys ran faster than ever. Jeremy reached the door first. The palms of his hands slammed down on the safety bar. The door swung open, the cool evening air blowing in his face. Behind them Worm screeched into the transmitter.

"They're getting out the back way. Stop them!"

The emergency exit of the Comedy Theatre opened into a narrow alley. The discolored bricks of the building itself hemmed it in on one side, a rusting metal fence stretching along the other. The alley led back down into the street, but even as the boys stopped to get their bearings, three men began to move slowly toward them. Nicholas could hardly believe what he was seeing. All of them carried guns.

There was no time to think. Following his brother, he ran in the opposite direction, following the alley to its end. And its end was abrupt. A brick wall ten feet high jutted out of the corner of the theater. It was too high to climb. They were trapped.

"Quick!"

Jeremy had cupped his hands and, hardly knowing what he was doing, Nicholas lifted his foot and allowed himself to be heaved upward. His head hit a loose brick, but then his hands were scrabbling for the top of the wall and he had pulled himself up. Squatting on the top, he turned to reach down for his brother.

"Jeremy!" he shouted.

Seeing what was happening, the three men had broken into a run.

"Jem . . . hurry!" He was almost sobbing the words.

His brother was standing on tiptoe, but the distance was too great. Their hands were inches apart. An eternity.

"Please, Jem!"

Nicholas felt his brother's fingertips brush his own. Blood

was running down his face. His eyes were wide and staring. He couldn't reach the hand.

Jeremy jumped, grabbing at him, then fell back.

"Go, Nick! Go!" he shouted.

Then the three men were on him. One raised his gun, then brought it down, cracking it against the back of Jeremy's head. At the same moment Nicholas staggered back and disappeared over the wall.

Inside the theater Worm lowered the radio transmitter. He licked his lips. A muscle under one eye was twitching. Mr. Banes was walking toward him, Don White close behind. Worm swallowed hard.

"We have one of them," he said at last. "But I'm sorry, Mr. Banes. The other got away."

There was a long silence, broken by the sound of Don White flicking a match to light another cigar. "You'll get him," he said. "But I've done my part of the deal. You owe me fifteen thousand dollars—as agreed."

Mr. Banes turned to look at him, his eyes behind the two coins of glass quite blank. "Oh, yes," he whispered. "We'll get the other one. An hour from now, every cop in New York will be looking for him. He'll be wanted for murder."

Don White smiled. "That's a great idea," he said. "A frame-up. That's terrific. . . ." A second thought crossed his mind. "Whose murder?" he asked.

The gun had appeared in Mr. Banes's hand as if by magic.

"Yours," he said.

He fired twice. Don White was hurled off his feet, crashing into the wall and sliding to the floor. His dead eyes gazed at Mr. Banes in outrage. The cigar still jutted out of his teeth, smoke curling upward.

Mr. Banes pushed the gun back into his holster.

"Let's get out of here," he said.

= THREE =

Linda Thorn

NICHOLAS HAD FALLEN awkwardly on the other side of the wall. Pulling himself to his feet, he limped away from the theater, pushing through the crowds and letting the city swallow him up. DONT WALK . . . DONT WALK. The traffic lights flashed at him in angry red, but he ignored them, stepping off the pavement without looking left or right. A large yellow taxi swerved to avoid him. The blare of its horn hit him like a fist and a string of angry threats rang in his ears. But then he had crossed the street and was once again following the sidewalk, not caring where it led him, thankful only for every inch that he could put between him and the theater.

Whatever happens, Nick . . . I'm your brother. I always will be.

Jeremy had known something was going to happen. He had known it from the moment they had arrived in New York and he had seen it, in some sort of vision, on the stage. The power, telepathy or whatever you liked to call it, had behaved in a way that was completely new, and that scared Nicholas even more than the events of the past thirty minutes. He remembered the look on his brother's face when he pulled off the mask. Jeremy had been terrified, on the edge of madness. What had he seen? Whatever it was, it had taken him.

Nicholas wiped some of the blood from his forehead and stared vaguely at the red stain on the palm of his hand. His thoughts went back to that moment on the wall. For a second time he saw his brother reaching out for him, saw the gun crashing down against his head. There was nothing he could have done. He had to get away. But with a wave of despair,

Nicholas knew that wasn't true. As ever, Jeremy had been there to protect him. He could have jumped down. Together they could have fought the men. But as ever, he had been too weak. His brother had needed help and he had failed him.

The street that he was following came to a crossroads and Nicholas paused, unsure which direction to take. The heart of Greenwich Village, with its bright lights, bars, and boutiques lay behind him now. Straight ahead, the way was darker, quieter. Where would he be safer? At least in the middle of the crowd the men would have more difficulty taking him, but in a strange way he almost wanted to be taken. He wanted to see Jeremy, to tell him he was sorry. The traffic lights changed. The single word WALK flashed in white. Automatically he obeyed, continuing into the shadows.

He had walked for another two minutes before he realized that he was being followed. There were footsteps about twenty yards behind him, but when he stopped to look back, there was nobody in sight. He pressed forward and almost at once the footsteps began again, a clattering echo of his own. Almost unconsciously he found himself quickening his pace, now taking a left turn, now a right, wishing that he could find his way back to the precarious safety of the crowd.

He had lost himself in a maze of twisting streets, the shops far behind him. For all Nicholas knew, he could have been retracing his steps back to the theater, but he could only go on. Seeing an open space ahead of him, he made for it, his heart sinking as he heard the footsteps strike up in pursuit.

The open space was Washington Square. A sign on the corner told him this, but left him none the wiser. It was rectangular in shape and dominated by a large stone archway. Concrete paths led across the grass and through the scattered trees. To one side was a fountain, silent and still, surrounded by benches. There were a few people in the area, but they weren't the sort of people he had hoped to meet.

A drunk lay asleep on a bench, his hands clutching a threadbare coat. A group of punks in torn jeans and dirty T-shirts skulked near the fountain, talking in low voices. They turned as Nicholas crossed the grass and sat down on a bench. His foot was hurting him now. He had to rest.

"You looking for something?"

Two of the punks had rolled over to him—rolled, because

they were wearing skates. Everything about them spelled trouble—the ugly way they looked at him, the bulge of knives in their back pockets.

"I'm all right," Nicholas said in a voice so thin that he could hardly recognize it as his own.

The two men looked at each other and smiled.

"Maybe he's run away from home," one said.

The other laughed. "And maybe he's got money—"

"Leave him alone!"

The voice had come from directly behind them. Nicholas looked past them, but all he could see was a young woman dressed in gray slacks and a red shirt, holding a handbag.

"Leave him alone," she said again.

"You his sister?" one of the boys asked.

By way of an answer the girl opened her handbag and drew out a small silver canister. "Listen," she said. "This is tear gas. It can blind you at six paces. And I'm a black belt in karate. So if I were you, I'd beat it."

The two boys hesitated for a moment, eyeing her curiously. Then they shrugged and roller-skated back to their friends.

As the woman slid the canister back into her handbag, Nicholas looked at her more closely. She was about twenty years old, short and wiry, with long black hair and freckles. She was wearing large pink glasses. A gold chain around her neck was her only jewelry. He wondered if he had seen her somewhere before. Her face was familiar, but he couldn't place her.

"You were following me," he said.

"You mean . . . you heard me?"

"Yes."

The woman sighed. "You weren't meant to. And I thought I was being so quiet! It must have been the high heels. . . ."

"Who are you?" Nicholas demanded.

"My name's Linda Thorn. I was in the theater tonight. Don't you remember me? I was the one with the key. You're Jeremy, aren't you?"

"No. I'm Nicholas." Suddenly he was angry. "I'm Nicholas. They took Jeremy. They—" He took a deep breath. Suddenly he didn't want to talk to this woman. He didn't want to talk to anyone.

"I'm sorry," Linda said. She sat down beside him. "That

was stupid of me. But you two, you're so alike. And in the costumes . . ." She sighed for a second time. "I'm sorry."

"What do you want?" Nicholas asked. His voice was still hostile.

"I want to help."

"How?"

"Well, I can offer you somewhere to stay for a start. You don't look to me as though you're about to check into the Waldorf-Astoria." The woman glanced nervously around her. "And I may be able to help you find out what happened to your brother."

"What do you know?" Nicholas asked.

Linda gestured at the group of skaters. They were still there, talking among themselves, occasionally looking back in their direction. "Let's move," she said. "Before they take any more interest in us."

"What about the tear gas?"

"It isn't tear gas. It's hair spray. And as for karate, the only chops I know anything about are the pork variety. Do you want to go?"

"Where?"

"I live on Amsterdam and One Hundred and Sixteenth Street on the Upper West Side." Nicholas made no reply so she added, "You can trust me."

"I don't know that." Nicholas stood up. "But I don't have any choice," he said.

The subway station was dark and dirty, virtually empty at that time of night. They waited on the littered platform beside an advertisement peeling at the corners. Nicholas read it, hardly taking in the words.

EVERY CHILD SHALL HAVE A BIBLE

Help bring sanity back into the world.

$35 pays for the printing and free distribution of one Bible to a child who needs it.

Mrs. E. Carnitt needs your support now. Pay for a Bible and help educate America.

The train, when it arrived, was dark and ancient, just about every inch of it covered with graffiti. Inside it was just the same. The walls, the ceiling, even the seats were a spider's web of black spray paint. As the train roared through the tunnels, Nicholas closed his eyes and tried to relax. But he couldn't. Everything was happening too quickly.

He was relieved when they arrived at the 116th Street subway station. They walked another few minutes, stopping finally at a brownstone in a quiet tree-lined street. Linda took out a bunch of keys. There were three locks on the front door alone.

"I'm afraid it's six floors up," she said. "And there's no elevator. Your foot okay?"

"It's okay," Nicholas said.

A winding staircase led up past a series of landings and doors. Linda lived on the top floor, Apartment 13. Two more locks, and they were in.

Paper. That was the first thing that Nicholas saw. In the center of the room there was a table piled high with sheets of paper. They were spilling out of an ancient typewriter too. Crumpled balls of paper grew like a crazy fungus out of a plastic wastebasket underneath the table. There were boxes of paper on the shelves, bundles of paper on the sofa and chairs, untidy heaps of paper on the floor.

No pictures hung on the walls. Instead, sheets of paper of different sizes had been stuck up with pins or Scotchtape. Nicholas glanced at one. It was a letter from a New York publisher, thanking her for her manuscript (*A Deadly Day in June*) but regretting that they were unable to consider it for publication. A dozen similar letters hung around it.

"I'm a writer," Linda said as she closed the door. "But I'm not very successful."

"What do you write?" Nicholas asked.

"Detective stories . . . thrillers." Linda went into the kitchen. "You must be hungry. How do you fancy some nut loaf?" She grinned apologetically. "I'm a vegetarian," she explained.

"No thanks."

"How about some herbal tea?"

"No." Nicholas shook his head.

"Do you want to get some sleep?"

Nicholas nodded gratefully. "That's all I want," he said.

"I don't know who you are. I don't know why you've helped me. But I can't talk . . . not now. I just have to be alone."

"No problem. We can talk in the morning." Linda went into the bedroom, returning for a moment later with a pillow and a pile of blankets. She scooped the papers off the couch and began to prepare a makeshift bed. "There's only one bed," she said as she worked, "so you'll have to sleep out here." She finished folding the blankets and straightened up. "There you go. You're sure you don't want me to look at your ankle?"

"No. It's all right."

"Fine. We'll talk in the morning." She went to the bedroom door. "Don't worry about things, Nicholas," she said. "I'm sure it's going to be okay."

"I hope so. . . ."

"Good night."

"Good night. And . . . Linda. Thanks."

She smiled at him and closed the door behind her. Nicholas undressed, then turned off the light and curled up under the blankets.

But he didn't sleep.

He had been waiting for Linda to go, to leave him by himself. There was something he wanted to try. Now he closed his eyes, relaxing his body against the cushions, trying to ignore the prickle of the blankets against his naked skin. His breathing became deep and steady. All his consciousness was focused on a point somewhere in the center of his forehead.

And then it was as if he had left his own body lying on the couch in Linda's apartment. He was all mind. He felt himself traveling through the great darkness, passing through brick and stone, soaring across the city of New York. Jeremy was near. He knew it. If he could join with him, become one with him, then he would know where they were taking him.

He could hear traffic, and something else. It was the whir of a machine, like a metal wheel turning. The wheel stopped with a loud click. A metal door clanged open and Nicholas shuddered as a hand pressed against his back and pushed him forward. The door closed again. The wheel turned. Where were they? Nicholas had no idea, but with an inner thrill he realized that they hadn't left New York. There wouldn't have been time. Wherever Jeremy was being taken, it was somewhere inside the city.

But something strange was happening. Involuntarily Nicholas reached out and grabbed hold of the sides of the sofa. The floor was swaying underneath him. They were no longer on the ground. An airplane? No. He had felt none of the rush of takeoff, and if it had been a helicopter, he would have heard the swish of the blades. But there was only a distant creaking somewhere above his head and a brief rattle at regular intervals.

"What's he doing?"

"I don't know, Mr. Banes."

A face appeared, staring at him curiously. Nicholas had never experienced anything like this before, and even at that moment he wondered what had happened to make his power grow so suddenly. It was as if Jeremy's eyes had become windows. He was looking through them. The face was staring at Jeremy. But Nicholas was the one who stared back.

He knew that face: the gray skin, the mustache, the hearing aid. Now Mr. Banes was looking at him with growing suspicion, the eyes narrow behind the round glasses. He seemed to come to a decision. Nicholas saw him raise a hand, flinched as it swept through the air. Jeremy was knocked off his feet, but it was Nicholas who felt the blow. His whole body recoiled. And then he was awake, still in Linda's apartment, the blankets in a tangle at his feet.

Slowly he got to his feet, groped for the light switch, and turned it on. There was a mirror hanging in the kitchen and he went over to it. Gingerly he rubbed his cheek just below his eye. There, sure enough, was a red mark, the skin puffing up. He could feel it throbbing under his fingertips. But still he smiled.

Jeremy was a prisoner, but he was alive. And he was in New York.

Somehow Nicholas would find him.

= FOUR =

Missing

NICHOLAS WAS AWAKENED by the smell of cooking. For a minute he blinked, wondering where he was. Then he saw some of the paper scattered around the couch and remembered.

"It's ten o'clock," Linda said. "I thought you were never going to wake up."

She was standing in the kitchen, turning what looked like two squashed pancakes over in a pan. "They're bean curd," she explained. "Less cholesterol than eggs. There's also salt-free wholemeal toast, skimmed milk, and decaffeinated coffee." She turned down the flame on the stove. "I like to look after myself," she added.

"I can see that," Nicholas said.

Linda had already been shopping, and ten minutes later, when Nicholas sat down at the breakfast bar that divided the kitchen from the living room, he was wearing new jeans and a cotton shirt. He ate a healthy breakfast—in more than one sense—and if the ingredients were a little unusual, he was too hungry to notice.

As she refilled his cup for a second time, Linda looked at Nicholas curiously. "What happened to you last night?" she asked.

"What?" Nicholas raised a hand and touched the bruise under his eye. "Oh . . . that! It's nothing. I must have fallen out of bed."

Linda shook her head in disbelief but asked no more questions. As soon as he finished eating, she piled the plates in the sink, then sat down next to him. Nicholas picked up a sheet of paper.

"Have you been writing for a long time?" he asked.

"About six years," Linda told him. "That's a page from *A Deadly Day in June*. It was turned down by seventy-four publishers. Now I'm working on a sequel."

"What's it called?"

"*A Deadly Day in July*." she sipped coffee. "I wanted to be a detective when I was younger, but since I couldn't do that, I became a detective writer." She sighed. "But it looks like I can't do that either."

Nicholas put down his cup. "It was good of you to put me up," he said. "But I'd better get moving now."

"Moving? Where?"

Nicholas shrugged. "I don't know. I have to find Jeremy. That's all."

"Where will you start?"

"He's in New York. . . ."

"You can't be sure of that."

Nicholas shook his head. "I am sure. I'll find him."

"Alone?"

"I am alone."

"What about me?"

There was a moment's silence. Then Linda stood up and went into the kitchen. "All right," she said. "Go ahead and walk out of here. Do you know how long I give you before you end up in jail? About five minutes." She picked up a newspaper. "I bought this when I went out," she continued. "It's the *Daily News*. Today's edition." She walked back and threw it in front of him. "Congratulations. You made the front page."

Nicholas looked down, his eyes widening in shock.

There was a photograph of him, taken at a performance in Boston. Above it was the headline: "TELEPATHIC" TWIN IN MURDER MYSTERY. He read the story:

> A bizarre shooting took place last night at the Comedy Theatre in Greenwich Village. The victim was 50-year-old Don White, impresario and businessman. Eyewitness accounts put the finger firmly on 14-year-old Nicholas Helsey.

White was shot twice at close range with a Browning 9mm automatic pistol. Death was instantaneous. There is no apparent motive for the killing. Don White was the manager of an off-Broadway cabaret called "Out of this World," purporting to be an exploration of the paranormal. In fact, Nicholas and his twin brother, Jeremy, used an elaborate system of signals to present a phony mind-reading act. Both boys were in White's care following the death of their parents four years ago in England.

Last night young Nicholas Helsey vanished without a trace, but police have advised the public to be on the lookout for him. Jeremy Helsey, now being cared for by friends of White's, released a statement in which he warned that his brother had recently been experimenting with narcotics and this may explain the killing. "Nicholas doesn't know what he's doing," the statement reads. "I'm afraid he may be a danger to anyone he comes into contact with."

Police have launched a citywide search for the boy, who is described as being of average height, thin, with light brown hair and brown eyes.

Nicholas put the newspaper down slowly. "So they killed Uncle Don," he said.

"I'm sorry . . ." Linda began.

"Don't be. He deserved it." Nicholas looked at the article again, his eyes drawn to the headline with its bold, accusing letters.

"It's a neat piece of work," Linda said. "In just four paragraphs they've made you a fraud, a drug addict, and a potential psychopath. It's the sort of stuff I write myself, only nobody ever prints it."

"Nobody's going to believe it," Nicholas said.

"Everyone will believe it." Linda reached out and took hold of him. "Don't you see? If you leave here alone, you won't stand a chance. Right now any boy alone in New York is going to be up for grabs."

"But with you . . . ?"

"You could be my kid brother. Why won't you let me help you, Nicholas?"

"I don't even know you!" Nicholas broke free. "Why should you get involved?"

"Involved?" Linda smiled. "I was involved long before I met you, Nicholas. Believe me—I'm involved."

Mr. Banes turned the volume control on his hearing aid almost to full and dialed a telephone number. An armed guard walked past outside his office, crossing the lawn between two of the buildings. Mr. Banes had ordered security to be tightened since the new boy had arrived. He had made one mistake. He couldn't afford another.

There was a click as someone picked up the phone on the other end. Mr. Banes uttered a single word.

"Banes."

"My dear Mr. Banes! It would appear that you have let me down."

It was cool in the room, but sweat had broken out on Mr. Banes's forehead. It clung to his gray skin like raindrops on a dirty window.

"We have one of them," he said. "But the other—somehow they knew that we were coming."

"Of course they knew!" The voice was shrill, unforgiving. "I warned you that when we found them, they would have power far beyond your shallow imagining. If they hadn't known, they would be of no interest to me. But even so, with a dozen men at your disposal, you allowed them to get the better of you."

Mr. Banes wished now that he hadn't turned the hearing aid up quite so high. The voice was boring into his brain. He could feel a pulse beating behind his eyes.

"The police will find the other one for us," he said. "I arranged it so—"

"I am not interested in your infantile arrangements!" The voice cut like a knife through his head. "Find the other boy and kill him."

"But—"

"Do you question me, Mr. Banes?"

"No! No! Of course not!" The sweat was trickling down his cheeks now. His collar was almost strangling him.

"If Jeremy Helsey is what I suspect he is, then I will have found what I have been looking for and it won't matter to me whether his brother lives or dies. If not, then both the boys will be useless to me."

"What do you want done with Jeremy?" Mr. Banes asked.

"You have him under sedation?"

"Yes."

"Good." The voice chuckled cruelly. "That should put an end to any telepathic communication between them. Keep him that way for two days, until I arrive."

"And then?"

"And then the treatment will begin."

Nicholas and Linda were walking through Central Park, the great stretch of grass and trees that stands like an oasis of calm in the bustle of Manhattan. It was a beautiful day, the sun glinting behind the distant towers of the skyscrapers. Birds were singing in the trees. Children played with boats on the pond. Couples strolled along the winding paths. In Central Park, everything was peaceful.

Even so, Nicholas couldn't relax. A policeman walking in the opposite direction passed close to them and he felt his stomach tighten. But the policeman took no notice of them. Linda had been right. They were looking for a boy on his own, not out walking with a woman who could be his big sister. And his appearance had changed since the newspaper with his photograph had been published. A bottle of dye had left his hair several shades darker, and he now wore a pair of glasses. They were simple devices, but together they added up to somebody who definitely wasn't Nicholas Helsey.

"I've lived nine years in New York. I'm twenty-seven now. Luckily I inherited money when I was young, and that's how I've supported myself." Linda sighed. "I still hope I'll get a break with my writing. But when you've been turned down by seventy-four publishers, I guess you have to start wondering."

They had reached a circular glade in the park. There was a statue in the middle of it: Alice, sitting on a toadstool, surrounded by some of the creatures from Wonderland. Nobody else was in sight. Linda chose a niche in front of a hedge and sat down, sliding her briefcase onto her lap.

"I came from Houston originally," she went on. "Anyway, there was a kid I knew out there. There was a time when I used to baby-sit for him. His name was Joe Fanelli. He was a nice kid . . . you know, straightforward, hardworking, and all that. But there was one thing—" Linda paused, searching for the words to express herself. "He used to have these flashes. It didn't happen often, but it was as if he were seeing into the future. For example, he might come down to breakfast and say "lucky double," and that wouldn't make any sense. But then later the same day there would be a horserace and a complete outsider called Lucky Double would win. It was that sort of thing. Always unexpected, uncontrolled. There were a couple of pieces about him in the local paper. He even went on the radio once.

"Well, about six months ago Joe disappeared. He would have been your age then. Perhaps a year younger. His parents managed to trace him as far as New York, and they came here, looking for him. Of course, I saw them. They stayed here a couple of months, but there was nothing they could do, so, in the end, they went back home again. But they asked me to look out for Joe, as if I'd bump into him on a street corner or something. And that, I thought, was that.

"Except that a week later Joe turned up. He was found floating in the East River and his whole arm was a mass of punctures. A heroin addict—that's what he'd become and that's what had killed him. I had to go down to the police station to identify him." She grimaced. "It was him, all right. God knows, I'll never forget it. . . .

"They flew the body home and buried him and I suppose in time they forgot about him. But for me it just didn't add up. I'd known Joe. There was no way he'd leave home, no way he'd poison himself with drugs. And there was something else."

She opened the briefcase and took out a scrap of paper. "They found this in his back pocket," she said. She handed it to Nicholas. "I kept it. I don't know why. Nobody else seemed to think it meant anything."

Nicholas looked at it. It was a page from a book, jagged and torn on one side, cut straight on the other three. The page was creased and dirty, a grim reminder of the river that had become Joe's grave. Most of the words were unreadable, but Nicholas managed to make out a few fragments.

". . . had in her hand a golden cup, full of abominations and the unclean things . . . the great, the mother . . . I saw her . . . the secret meaning of the woman . . ."

"What is it?" Nicholas asked.

"It's a page from the Bible," Linda told him. "It comes from the Revelation of St. John. I bought a Bible and read it, but I'm afraid it doesn't make much more sense than the piece you have."

"But why . . . ?"

"Exactly." Linda took the page back. "Tell me Joe's left home. Tell me he became an addict. But why should he have a page from the Bible in his back pocket? It doesn't add up." She reached into the briefcase again and took out a thick file. "So I started to do some research," she continued. "I tell you, Nicholas, you wouldn't believe how many children are missing in New York. There are hundreds of them a year. There's an organization—Childfind—that's been set up to look for them. But it's hopeless. The situation's gotten so bad that they've started sticking photographs of lost kids on telephone poles. They even print them on milk cartons, for God's sake!"

"What happens to these children?" Nicholas asked.

"Some of them are murdered. Perhaps they're the lucky ones. Others get drawn into drugs, delinquency . . . and worse. But I came across something really strange." She opened the file. "In the last few months about twenty-five percent of the children who have been missing have had powers like Joe's." She glanced at Nicholas. "Like yours. Look at this." She started turning pages. "This kid was believed to be able to move things with the power of thought. This girl was a pyrokinetic . . . a firestarter. This one here was a faith healer. This next one got messages from the dead." She flicked through the file. "All children. All with paranormal abilities. All missing."

"Who's this one?"

Nicholas pointed to the back of the folder, where there was a page cut out of an English newspaper. It showed a photograph of a young boy and it had caught his eye because for a minute he had thought he was looking at Jeremy. A headline just below the photograph read: DID SCHOOLBOY SEE INTO THE FUTURE?

"Oh, him!" Linda said. "He's different. At least, he hasn't exactly disappeared. His name's Martin Hopkins. He was involved in some pretty weird goings-on in Yorkshire. But I've heard he's in Peru now."

She closed the file.

"There's nothing conclusive," she said. "But it looks to me as if someone is kidnapping these children."

"Why haven't you gone to the police?"

"I have gone to the police—a dozen times. They just think I'm a failed thriller writer with too much imagination. I've been forced to go on alone. That's why I was at the theater last night. When I saw you and Jeremy were performing, I knew something was going to happen. And I was right."

"It all hangs together," Nicholas agreed. "Even the drugs. . . . It said in the newspaper that I was taking drugs. Like Joe, I suppose." He stood up and walked over to the statue, resting his hand on the Mad Hatter's shoulder. "But why?" he exclaimed. "What do they want us for? And who are they?"

"Jeremy could probably tell us that," Linda said.

And suddenly Nicholas was back on the wall once again. The gun swung down. The three men closed in.

"Jeremy . . ." he whispered.

= FIVE =

The Island

JEREMY STILL COULDN'T believe it. He was standing no more than five hundred yards away from the headquarters of the United Nations. He could clearly see the great green tower and the lower, gently curving General Assembly Building. He could even make out some of the flags fluttering outside—the Union Jack, the Stars and Stripes, the Tricolor of France, and the Maple Leaf of Canada. But he was in another world.

A wide expanse of muddy water—the East River—separated him from the building. Long flat barges cruised up and down throughout the day, carrying goods and machinery to the New York ports. They kept their distance from the island, warned off by a series of red buoys, but Jeremy wondered if the captain or crew ever looked toward the island, ever paused to wonder what might be going on there. Perhaps one of them might be training his binoculars on him even now. He could make some sort of signal. . . .

But he knew it would do no good. He would be ignored by the captain and punished by the guards. The island's cover was too perfect.

A maximum security prison covered about one third of the island, cut off from the rest by an electrified barbed wire fence. This was the part he was in now. Swimming away was impossible. Each of the three sides was guarded by a watch-tower equipped with spotlight and submachine gun—and even without them, the currents were too dangerous, the distance too great.

Apart from the watchtowers, the compound was made up of four buildings. Right at the front by the main gate stood Block A, the largest of the four. It was an ugly place, five stories high, its gray brick facade punctuated by lines of barred windows. From the front it looked like a hospital. From the back it was more like a castle, complete with battlements and circular corners like barbicans. Once, Jeremy had been told, it had been a lunatic asylum. The cold hand of madness still clung to every brick.

Now it was a prison for about three hundred children, aged ten to eighteen. There was nothing fake about the prison. Its inmates had been sentenced by the courts for crimes ranging from truancy and running away to violent theft and even murder. Block A had its own exercise yard, its own laundry, dining hall, and workshop. It even had its own printing presses . . . filling the air with the whir of machinery from morning until night. But Jeremy had no idea just what was being printed there or why.

A muddy road led from the main gate, around Block A, and down past the guards' quarters to the end of the island. It was known as Gallows Way. About halfway down another road forked off, leading eventually to a parking lot. It was here that Block B was situated. This was a smaller version of the castle, built from the same bricks. At the moment it housed seventy children. They, too, were prisoners. But there was nothing ordinary about them.

Only a few of them had committed crimes, and none of them had been sent to the island by the courts. They had come from all over America. Some had been kidnapped, bundled into cars in the middle of the night. Some of them had been spirited away from orphanages or other government institutions. A few had been sold, like Jeremy, by guardians or relatives.

They all had one thing in common. At some time in their lives they had exhibited powers that went beyond the ordinary. A newspaper might pick up the story. Their name might be mentioned on TV or radio. A short while later they would disappear.

The "specials," as they were called, were given the run of the compound. They could walk across the lawns, throw Frisbees, watch the boats pass along the East River. They were never out of the sight of armed guards, patrolling on foot and manning the towers. They couldn't swim away. And if they made some sort of signal, anyone watching would just assume that they were ordinary prisoners, juvenile delinquents. And so, by day, they walked. But they avoided the southern tip of the island. Nobody passed through the clump of trees that separated it. For that was where the fourth building was located. The Treatment Center.

The Treatment Center was the main reason for the island's existence. It was a small building, the only one in the compound that was brand-new. It was built from black bricks. It had a single metal door and no windows. At intervals during the day loudspeakers mounted in the trees would crackle and the emotionless voice of Mr. Banes would call out: "Number one seven four to the Treatment Center," and somewhere, someone would go pale and his friends would turn away, thankful that it was not them.

In the end, however, all the specials would be called to the Treatment Center. They might be lucky. There were sessions that involved only tests. Can you tell me the design on this card without looking at it? Make this glass move without touching it. Sometimes they were told simply to go to sleep, a sleep monitored by softly glowing machines and blinking display units connected to their temples by a maze of colored wires. Mr. Banes was probing: searching for their power, encouraging it, measuring it. If there was nothing, if the power was too weak or sporadic, then the sessions would end. The specials would be transferred to Block A. That would be the end of it.

But when he probed more deeply, when he embarked on more deadly experiments, that was when the pain would begin. The Treatment Center was soundproofed so that nobody could hear the screams. Number 174 might be in there for an hour. He might be in there for a day. Perhaps he would never be seen again. The specials were always changing. Nobody had been in Block B longer than three months. New subjects were always arriving. And all of them were waiting, waiting for the time when their number would be called and their friends would move away from them as if afraid of being contaminated.

Jeremy stood on the edge of the river, gazing at the United

Nations. He had been on the island for three days now. They had taken his watch, so he had no idea of the exact time, but from the position of the sun he guessed it was about midday. He looked again at the water, poised to jump in, to swim across. He had always been a strong swimmer. Surely he could make it. A guard walked past along the path behind him, a rifle slung over his shoulder. It was hopeless. He would be shot before he had gone ten yards.

He remembered his arrival on the island. There had been a moment, on the way, when he had been aware of a familiar sensation and had felt a surge of hope. Nicholas had been there with him, inside him. Nicholas had gotten away and despite the distance between them, he had managed to make contact. He had been on the point of responding, telling him where they were taking him, when Mr. Banes had finished it, brutally slapping him across the face. But how much had Nicholas been able to see? Would it have been enough?

After that, they had taken him into an office in the guards' quarters, just behind Block A on Gallows Way. Mr. Banes had explained to him the rules of conduct on the island while two armed guards stood over him. He had been given a number—300. He would no longer have a name.

"From now on," Mr. Banes had said, "you will do exactly as you are told. If you disobey, you will be disciplined. Any attempt to escape from this island will be punished by death. Do you understand?"

"Yes."

"Yes, *sir*."

"Yes . . . sir."

But that hadn't been the end of it. Mr. Banes had opened a drawer in his desk and taken out a bottle of red capsules. He had held one out in the palm of his hand.

"Now you will take this," he had instructed.

Jeremy had hesitated, unsure which revolted him more, the gleaming red capsule, or the dead gray flesh on which it rested.

"You will obey, number three hundred!" Mr. Banes had snapped. "If you will not take it of your own accord, I will have your mouth forced open and the capsule pushed down your throat."

So Jeremy had taken it. Somehow he had managed to swallow it. There had been no choice.

Since then there had been more capsules: one every morning, one every night. He could feel their effect now. He was slow and lethargic. The capsules had confused him, making it impossible to concentrate. He knew why he had been given them. In his present state of mind there could be no further communication with Nicholas. He was utterly alone.

Jeremy took one last, longing look at the United Nations. It was while his attention was fixed on the flags that the loudspeaker crackled and the dull, disinterested voice of Mr. Banes called out.

"Number three hundred to the Treatment Center. Number three hundred."

He closed his eyes. So now it was his turn. Briefly, Jeremy considered his options. He could refuse to go, but why prolong the inevitable? They would only come after him, hurt him for disobeying, and then drag him there anyway. There was nowhere to run to, nowhere to hide.

His legs were feeling weak and there was a sick hollow in his stomach. But there was nothing he could do. Slowly he crossed the lawn and began to follow Gallows Way down to the bottom of the island.

= SIX =

The Citadel

"YOU'RE SURE IT was the Citadel?"

"I'm positive."

"Positive?"

"Sure I'm positive."

Nicholas and Linda were walking down Fifth Avenue, following the only clue they had. Nicholas had gone over the events in the Comedy Theatre over and over again. He was at the back of the auditorium. Jeremy was on the stage. There was a man with blond hair and strangely repulsive muscles. Briefly, their hands had touched. That was when it had all begun: Jeremy's vision, the nightmare chase. And the man had shown him a security pass with a photograph, a name, and an address. Albert Worm. The Citadel, New York.

For two days now they had been going to the Citadel, sitting at the coffee bar, drinking as many cups as Linda could afford. At two dollars a round, that wasn't many. But as Nicholas had said, if the man with yellow hair worked there, they might spot him. If they spotted him, they could follow him. And if they followed him, he might lead them to Jeremy.

"How do you know he had anything to do with it?" Linda had asked the evening before over a supper of lentil and brown rice casserole.

Nicholas had been unable to answer. He hadn't seen the man among those who had chased him. He could have been a perfectly innocent member of the audience. All he had to go on was that single moment of contact and the way the man had flinched, as if afraid of being seen.

He was desperate, clutching at straws—and he knew it. But what else could he do? What other hope was there?

Now they reached the end of Central Park and crossed Fifth Avenue. Once again the Citadel rose up before them. Despite his mood, Nicholas couldn't help marveling at the building, the newest addition to the Manhattan skyline.

Designed by an unknown architect, it was ninety-two stories high, only ten less than the famous Empire State Building It had been completed in just fifty-two weeks, exactly a year. This was more than a feat of engineering. It was an impossibility. New Yorkers had watched it spring upward like a fabulous plant, and even in a city where people are used to being impressed, they had paused and raised their eyebrows.

The Citadel had been opened by the mayor of New York himself. In his inaugural speech, he had referred to the building as the Silver Citadel, for it was indeed silver from tip to toe. Even the windows, dazzlingly reflecting the sun, could have been fashioned from sheets of polished metal. The name had stuck. Though still "the Citadel" to the post office and city authorities, it was "the Silver Citadel" to everyone else.

And it was a fantastic building, its architecture quite unique. It was narrowest not at the top, where you'd expect, but at the bottom. The first fifteen floors formed a cylinder less than a hundred yards in diameter. On top of these, the next two floors jutted out in a wide circle. The remaining seventy-five floors, slightly wider than the base, soared up toward the sky, tapering to a point only at the very top, which was crowned by a glittering steel tower, a needle pricking at the sky.

As Nicholas and Linda approached the front entrance, the door slid open silently. They were greeted by the sound of piano music, played by an elderly musician seated at a baby grand in the foyer. The Citadel was just as impressive inside as outside. Glittering silver darkened into deep black. Smoked glass lined the walls. Black marble covered the floor. The two colors came together in the uniforms of the receptionists and porters, who welcomed visitors with polite smiles.

The lower fifteen floors had been designed like an Elizabethan theater, with a wide courtyard in the center. Real trees had been planted at the bottom. In the middle a fountain rose, the water glistening silver, too, against the dark green leaves. Escalators led them fifteen floors up to a circular gallery that was given over to lounges, coffee bars, restaurants, and shops.

Once again Linda and Nicholas took their places in the coffee bar from where they could see just about everyone who came in or left the building. Above them there were offices. The escalators surrounded them. The elevators—round tubes gliding soundlessly on silver rods—were transparent. If the man with yellow hair did make an appearance, they would have every chance of seeing him.

Linda ordered two coffees from a white-coated waiter.

"I should have brought a thermos bottle," she muttered once he had gone.

"I don't even want a coffee," Nicholas said.

"Nor do I," Linda agreed. "But if we don't have something, we'll be told to leave. These seats are worth money."

Time passed. The coffee was served and sipped as slowly as possible. More coffee was ordered. The elderly pianist was relieved by a younger woman, who began to play the same tunes all over again, only faster. People came and went. Never once did Nicholas stop searching through the building, hoping to catch a sight of the man he had come to find.

"Linda. . . ?"

"Yes?" Linda glanced upward. It had been ten minutes since Nicholas had spoken.

"I just wanted to say . . . it's kind of you to help me."

"Forget it." Linda shrugged. "I've got nothing else to do."

"What about your books?"

"My books? Nobody's interested in my books. My parents keep on hoping I'll give them up and settle down and get married."

"Why don't you?"

Linda smiled. "For the same reason why I'll never be a writer. Too many rejections." She stood up. "All this coffee!" she exclaimed. "I need to powder my nose. See you in a couple of minutes."

Nicholas watched her disappear in the direction of the ladies' room. He had looked at a couple of pages from her novel in the apartment and couldn't help but feel that she was the worst writer he had ever read. Even her shopping lists hardly made any sense. But in the few days that he had been staying with her, he had grown to like her. And right now she was the only friend he had. Smiling, he turned back . . . and froze.

One of the elevators was reaching the gallery level. There were only two people in it, a woman carrying a shopping bag and a man dressed in black leather trousers and a T-shirt. The man stared blankly into space. His hand reached up and brushed the yellow hair out of his eyes. Albert Worm. Even if he hadn't been wearing the same clothes, Nicholas would have recognized him.

Frantically, he looked back, hoping to call out to Linda. But she had already gone. He thought of chasing her, but the elevator was moving too rapidly. He was fifteen stories up with only an escalator to carry him down to ground level. If he hesitated, the man would get away. He stood up. He and Linda had made an arrangement in case they got separated. When she got back and found him gone, she would know what to do.

As the waiter arrived carrying fresh cups of coffee, Nicholas ran for the escalator. Ignoring the cries of a woman and her dog as Nicholas slammed into them, knocking them down, he let nothing stop him. Propelled by the momentum of the escalator, he leaped down, three steps at a time, swerving around the corners at the bottom of every flight and skidding onto the next. The elevator had already reached ground level. Nicholas saw the door open. Worm got out. Nicholas still had seven stories to go.

Nicholas took four steps in one jump, missed his footing, and nearly threw himself over the edge of the terrace. The handrail slammed into his chest and he reeled back, only to leap onto the next escalator, forcing his way past the shoppers and businessmen who got in his way. Somebody tried to stop him, clutching his shoulder, but he shook the hand off. There were three stories to go, but Worm was already out of sight.

At last he reached the bottom and sprinted across the reception area. Dodging to avoid a porter, he collided with the pianist. A resounding discord clanged through the building. Without pausing to apologize, Nicholas hurtled toward the glass-plated doors. Even as he ran, he wondered if they would open in time. If they didn't, he would crash right through them, for it was too late to stop now. But with only inches to spare, the infra-red beam was activated and the doors slid aside. And then he was out on the street, searching left and right, trying to catch his breath.

For a moment he thought he had lost Worm. It was lunch-time and the street was crowded. Then he caught sight of him, lumbering through the crowd, his head swaying first to one side, then to the other. Worm was walking down Fifth Avenue to the south, away from Central Park. Nicholas was careful to keep a safe distance between them. It was unlikely that the man would turn around, but if he did, he would doubtless recognize Nicholas as quickly as Nicholas had recognized him. He paused at the corner and Nicholas was afraid that he was going to call a cab. He had only a couple of dimes and a quarter on him. Not even enough for a bus.

But then Worm crossed over and walked on down the next block. He did look back once—whether through some sixth sense of his own or because he was naturally cautious, Nicholas couldn't say. But even as Worm stopped, he ducked into the doorway of a bookshop. People passed in both directions. Satisfied, Worm continued on.

In this way they crossed six blocks together. Worm finally left Fifth Avenue at 51st Street, taking a right turn. Nicholas sprinted down to the corner just in time to see him enter a doorway on the other side of the street.

There was a telephone booth nearby. Nicholas went over to it, pushed a coin into the slot, and dialed a number. Linda had given it to him two days before—an emergency number in case they were separated. It was the number of a public telephone in the Citadel.

He finished dialing. The telephone rang once before it was answered.

"Nicholas?" It was Linda's voice.

"Linda . . ."

"What happened?"

"I saw the man . . . Worm. I've followed him."

"Are you sure it was him?"

"Yes."

"Where are you?"

Nicholas looked across the street. "I'm on Fifty-first Street," he said. "Outside a place called Radio City. The stage door. He just went in. I'm going in after him."

"Wait!" Linda cried. "Don't go in by yourself. I'll be with you in a few minutes. Wait for me where you are, Nicholas. Nicholas . . . ?"

But Nicholas had already crossed the street. He had left the phone hanging.

= SEVEN =

Under Radio City

THERE WAS A show due to start that afternoon at half past two and people were bustling in and out of the Radio City stage door: actors and actresses, musicians and dancers, technicians and stagehands. Nicholas joined a crowd of them hoping to pass in unnoticed, but he hadn't taken more than three paces when he was stopped by a man in a glass booth to the left of the stage door.

"Where are you going, son?" the man asked.

"I'm . . . er . . ." There was a staircase to one side of the narrow hallway and Nicholas wondered if he should make a dash for it. But then a second man, dressed in a dark blue uniform, appeared, walking toward him, blocking the way. "A man came in here just now," he said. "Blond hair . . . leather trousers."

"He went down to stage control," the security guard muttered.

"Why do you want him?" the first man asked.

Both men seemed to be staring at him suspiciously and Nicholas began to feel nervous. Despite the glasses and hair dye, he still felt very much like the boy whose photograph had been on the front page of just about every New York newspaper a few days before. Even as he stood there, he could feel his disguise crumbling. How long would it be before they recognized him? Suddenly he wanted to get out.

"It doesn't matter," he said. "He's just a friend. I'll catch him later."

He smiled weakly and backed out into the street, knocking into a woman who was on her way in with a pile of costumes. Nicholas apologized, smiled again, and hurried away. The two men shrugged and forgot about him.

It was only when he was outside in the street that he regretted his nervousness. If it had been Jeremy there, he would have brazened it out, thought up some clever story to get past. But Nicholas had just let himself be pushed aside. He had been given one lucky break—spotting Albert Worm in the Citadel—one chance to find his brother. And as ever he had failed.

He lingered beside a poster advertising the show that was due to start in less than an hour's time. It was called *The Children of God* and it was described as ". . . a celebration of the New Testament in words, music, and song, presented by Mrs. E. Carnitt for all the family . . ." Next to it, there was a photograph taken from the production. It showed an actor dressed as Jesus Christ, sitting on a donkey and surrounded by a group of children who looked as if they were all about to be sick. In fact, they had been photographed just as they burst into song. There was a caption underneath it from the Gospel of St. Matthew: "Suffer the children to come unto me . . ."

The picture gave Nicholas an idea. If there were child actors in the show, why couldn't he be one of them? He took off his glasses and brushed his hair forward. He would simply march in, pretending that he knew where he was going, and if anybody tried to stop him, he would say that he was an understudy, that he was heading for the stage. The minutes were ticking away. If there was still any hope of finding Worm inside the theater, he would have to act fast.

As it turned out, there was no need for any pretense. When Nicholas returned to the stage door, both the security guards were struggling with an enormous bouquet of flowers that had arrived for Mrs. Carnitt, the producer of the show. At the same time, another group of people—including three or four children—walked in, chatting among themselves. Nicholas allowed himself to be swept in with them. An elevator had just arrived opposite the glass booth and they all piled in. By the time the security guards looked around, the doors were already closing. The elevator shivered. Then, with a sigh of relief, Nicholas felt it descend. He was in.

The elevator stopped at the next floor and the rest of the people got out, heading for the dressing rooms. Nicholas reached out and pressed the bottom button. Worm had gone ". . . down to stage control. . . ." whatever that was. Nicholas didn't even know why a stage should need controlling. But the security guard had definitely said "down" and Nicholas was now as far down as he could get.

The doors slid open and Nicholas stepped out into a long, poorly lit corridor. One end led down to a set of double doors which turned out to be locked, so Nicholas tried the other end. The corridor was bare except for a fire hose and a paper sign pointing the way to the Musicians' Club Room. There was nobody in sight. About halfway down the hall, a staircase led back up again. As Nicholas passed it, he heard footsteps and the sound of men talking. He hurried along, turning a corner just as three men appeared, one of them carrying a metal toolbox. They paused at the bottom of the staircase. Nicholas watched them, the sound of his own heartbeat echoing in his ears. One of the men finished a joke. The other two laughed. Then they continued down the corridor back toward the double doors.

There was a second, short flight of stairs around the corner with a doorway on the right. Nicholas tried it, but that, too, was locked. He took the stairs, coming out in a broad passageway with a line of plain wooden crates on one side. A camel blinked at him from the shadows with two beady eyes. A camel? Nicholas looked again and smiled to himself. It was a stuffed camel, life-size and perfect in every detail. For a moment he had thought it was alive.

". . . so this guy turns to the gorilla and says . . ."

Two of the men he had seen on the stairs were coming back. Nicholas leaped over the crates and ducked down behind the camel as they approached, still telling jokes. Cautiously, he peered over the camel's hump. The two men walked past and disappeared through an archway.

He waited until he was quite sure they had gone, then continued forward, bare light bulbs set high in the ceiling marking his progress. If the first corridor had reminded him of an abandoned hospital, he now found himself in what looked like a bizarre factory. A low metal fence ran along the left-hand side of the passageway opposite the crates. Nicholas looked over it and down into a sunken area, about the size of a swimming pool. Could this be the stage control? If so, it had to be an extremely complicated stage.

The area was lined by a network of gray steel pipes, forming an intricate pattern across the floor. Some were thin, others thicker, all joining together at points marked by bright orange wheels like steering wheels. Gray and yellow girders had been mounted at intervals like tent supports, and there were six metal beds—at least that's what they looked like—mounted on springs and embedded in concrete. A number of smooth golden rods soared out of the floor, stretching as far as Nicholas could see. Black curtains and loops of cable hung down from the ceiling, which was made of wood though itself criss-crossed by steel supports. The whole area was lit by spotlights raised just above the ground, which cast a strange, almost radioactive light across the silent machinery.

As Nicholas paused, taking it all in, the sound of voices reached him. He looked around, but there was no one in sight. The sound seemed to be coming out of the ground. Carefully, one step at a time, he moved toward it. He recognized one of the voices, high-pitched and nasal. He had heard it before in the hypnotist's dressing room at the Comedy Theatre.

". . . it's coming in from Montreal."

"Eighty kilos?"

"That's right."

There was a trapdoor set in the floor with a metal ladder leading down. Nicholas crouched beside it and peered into a room that would not have looked out of place on a submarine. It was long and narrow, with no windows. Pipes and cables tracked across the ceiling. About half the room was taken up by metal cupboards, a desk, and a makeshift couch. The other half was given over to a bank of machinery: switches, valves, and fuses reaching from floor to ceiling.

Albert Worm was perched on the end of the desk, poking his nose with a pencil. The other man was standing opposite him, just out of Nicholas's range of vision. This second man spoke with a Spanish accent.

"Eighty kilos," he said. "And it's ninety-five percent pure."

"Do you know the suppliers?" Worm asked.

"Yes. You can trust them."

Worm crossed one leg over the other. "We're almost ready to move," he said. "This will be the last shipment."

"That's your concern, amigo," the man with the accent replied.

"Right." Worm had come to a decision. "Fulton. Tomorrow night. At one o'clock. Usual security."

Nicholas backed away as Worm slid off the desk and moved toward the ladder. He had understood very little of the conversation. Something was being brought from Montreal. Worm was going to buy it at a place called Fulton. Even as he filed these facts away in his memory, Nicholas felt a pang of disappointment. It had nothing to do with Jeremy. It had nothing to do with anything.

But there was still a chance that Worm might go on somewhere else. Nicholas ducked behind the archway as Worm appeared, headfirst out of the floor, pressing himself into the shadows. The other man had followed him out, and now they shook hands and went their separate ways.

Nicholas's shoulder was touching a ledge that ran along the wall behind him. As he leaned forward to spy on Worm, he must have touched a loose screw. For a moment he saw it rolling toward the edge of the shelf. He stretched out a hand to catch it, felt it strike the side of his fingers, watched it drop to the floor. It only made a small sound—a clink and a rattle—but in the stillness of the control area, it might just as well have been a thunderclap.

Worm must have heard it. Squinting through the darkness, Nicholas saw him stop on the passageway beside the sunken rectangle. He retraced a few steps. Nicholas froze. But then he shook his head as if dismissing the sound and casually walked on.

Nicholas waited a full minute before following him. There had to be another doorway leading back underneath the passage and obscured by the high angle. But when he reached the bottom, he found himself confronted by a plain brick wall with no doorway, no opening. So where had Worm gone? Nicholas took another two steps. The strange, frozen light cast a black shadow across the wall. Too late he saw that the shadow was not his own. Too late he realized that Worm had heard the screw fall, had tricked him into following him down.

The blow crashed into his side, just below the shoulder, hurling him into one of the golden pillars. Worm had kicked him with both feet at the same time, pivoting his body on one of the metal beds that had been hiding him. It was a feat of acrobatics that was as impressive as it was deadly. Nicholas slumped to the floor and watched, helpless, as the man walked toward him, crouched down like a deformed ape. He was smiling, the damp hair reaching down to his mouth.

"A spy!" he whispered. "An eavesdropper!"

He reached down with two clawlike hands and seized hold of Nicholas's shirt. Nicholas felt himself being dragged to his feet as though he were a sack of feathers. For a moment his face was only an inch away from Worm's. Worm giggled horribly, recognizing him.

"Nicholas Helsey!" He said. "Little Nicholas Helsey . . ."

The hands jerked and Nicholas was flying, impossibly, through the air. He saw a confusion of wheels and pipes rushing up at him. Instinctively his hands curled up to protect his head, and that was how he landed, a disjointed bundle that skidded across the floor and slammed into a tangle of machinery. The whole of one side, where he had been kicked, was numb. Desperately, he shook his head. The spotlights were dazzling him. He couldn't see.

But then, with a jolt of pure terror, he saw the squat silhouette of Worm, pushing his way through the glare as though it were a curtain. He opened his mouth to scream, but no sound would come. Worm was going to kill him, he knew it. The man was relentless, closing in an inch at a time, delaying the end only for his own amusement. Now he was humming to himself, the sound somewhere between a high-pitched tune and an insane laugh. The hands reached through the light, stretching out for his throat.

There was something underneath Nicholas, digging into his ribs. He pulled at it and it came loose. A crowbar. One of the stage technicians must have used it to loosen the wheels and left it there after finishing work. Worm stopped, hovering over him. With what was left of his strength, Nicholas swung upward and felt the iron bar bury itself in Worm's stomach.

An ordinary man would have been crippled or killed. But Worm was protected by layers of misplaced muscle. Even so, he let out a howl of pain and surprise, staggered back, and tripped over a valve set in the floor. Somehow Nicholas managed to stand up. He still clutched the crowbar in one hand. Worm was stretched out beneath him, one leg twisted beneath his body. Grimly, Nicholas raised the crowbar.

"Wait!" Worm's voice was a whisper, the word half-trapped in his throat. He coughed, holding out a beseeching hand. "You want your brother . . ." he gasped at last. "I can help you."

"Where is he?" Nicholas demanded. "What have you done with him?"

"Not far . . . wait!"

"Tell me now!"

"He's here . . . here!"

The hand flicked out. Nicholas followed it with his eyes. But once again it was a trick. Once again he was too slow. The hand was empty and while his attention was distracted, Worm moved with lightning speed. His foot flew up. It caught the side of his hand. The crowbar was kicked out of his grasp. Then Worm was on him.

There was nothing Nicholas could do. The man's fists were like battering rams. After the second blow Nicholas stopped even trying to defend himself. All the strength had drained out of him.

When Worm finished, Nicholas sat against the wall, his legs splayed, his head lolled to one side. He was still conscious, but unable to move. He watched as Worm paused, breathing heavily, and wiped away the blood from his nose. He made no attempt to resist as he was picked up for a second time and half-carried to the far corner of the rectangle. He could hear somebody groaning and was surprised to realize that it was himself. Worm threw him down onto one of the metal beds, and just for once it did feel like a bed. The hard surface could have been a mattress. Nicholas was happy to lie there. He wanted to sleep.

Worm left him there for a moment, returning with a coil of wire and a thick piece of rag. Too weak to move, Nicholas allowed his mouth to be opened, felt Worm force the material in. It tasted of dirt and oil. He tried to cry out only when Worm looped the wire over the rag and tied it underneath the bed, behind his head. But by then it was too late. The wire was inside his mouth, pressing the rag against the back of his throat and holding his head against the metal. He was unable to stand up.

Worm twisted the wire in a complicated knot and straightened up. Then he leaned over, his lips close to Nicholas's ear.

"You hit me," he hissed. "You hurt me. Now you'll pay for it." He pointed at the ceiling. "Watch that," he continued. "The show will start soon. That's the stage, there, above us. When they want to change the set, the stage will sink. It'll come down . . . slowly . . . inch by inch." Worm patted the metal bed. "When it reaches the bottom, it will rest on this support. It will rest on you . . . fifty tons of it. You'll be squashed so flat, they'll have to carry you out with a spoon."

Nicholas tried to speak, tried to raise his head. But the wire was tied too tight. Any movement only squeezed the rag further into his mouth, threatening to choke him. Worm grinned at him.

"You're going to die, little Nicholas Helsey," he said. "But slowly. You'll see death. You'll watch it coming. You'll wait for it. And when it finally arrives, you'll welcome it."

Worm took one last, gloating look at the prostrate body. Then he lumbered away, heading for the ladder. Far above him, the orchestra struck up.

The show had begun.

= EIGHT =

Stage Fright

THERE IS NO stage in the world quite like the one in Radio City Music Hall.

It is divided into three sections that can go up and down like giant elevators. But how many elevators do you know that can support the weight of a full orchestra with thirty-six musicians and two grand pianos? The Radio City stage can manage all this—and more.

The middle of the stage is also a turntable that can make a complete circle, although all three sections have to be absolutely level before it can rotate. This is controlled by one man, who keeps in constant radio contact from a small room far below. All the pipes and cables that Nicholas had seen are activated by him.

Scene changes can be made either on the stage itself or twenty-seven feet below, where an army of stagehands will be waiting to begin. While this is going on, the elevators will rest on metal beds, sprung and set in concrete. Even when they're empty, the three sections weigh almost two hundred tons, so the metal beds have to be strong.

It was to one of these beds that Nicholas was tied.

His whole body was hurting now. He could only just lift his left arm, and any movement seemed to turn a knife in his stomach. He wondered if some of his ribs had been broken, but didn't dare run a hand down his chest to find out. His shirt was damp—whether with sweat or blood he couldn't say. Worse still, he couldn't see. He was forced to stare straight up. His body was free. Only his head was tied.

Nicholas had understood only a little of what Worm had told him. He could hear the vague sound of the orchestra, and when the music finished, a burst of applause like a rumble of thunder before a storm. Then there was a loud grinding and he saw part of the ceiling—a circle in the very middle—begin to turn. This was the revolving stage. Nicholas rested, trying to channel some strength back into his battered limbs. It was only when the front section of the stage began it's descent that he realized the terrible danger that awaited him.

He was alerted by a loud buzzing and a click. All around him the machinery sprang to life. Yellow and gray levers sprang back as if pulled by invisible hands. Pipes running the full length of the rectangle began to turn. Cog connected with cog. Cables, looped in the air above him, coiled upward. Long black curtains unfurled themselves. And one third of the ceiling began its slow journey down, traveling on the golden pillars until it came to rest on three of the metal beds.

There was a huge gap in the ceiling where the stage had descended. Behind it, on the other two thirds, the performance would still be going on. Nicholas could just make out the blink of spotlights, suspended in the back of the auditorium and directed on the stage. They could have been a mile away. No light from the stage control area could seep out upward. That was why the black curtains had been automatically lowered. A man ran along a gangway midway between Nicholas and the stage. To Nicholas, he was no more than a pair of legs. Nicholas tried to call out. But the rag in his mouth stifled any sound, and in the gloomy corner of the basement, there was no chance that he would be seen.

The machinery clicked and buzzed again and the section began to climb back up. At the same time, the second section slid down, this time stopping halfway to the bottom. Three sections . . . Nicholas could count them now. And he understood. When the time came for the third section to make its journey down, he would be directly underneath it. He would be crushed.

With a surge of panic he curled back both his hands, his fingers tugging feverishly at the wire. But Worm had known what he was doing. No matter how much he stretched, the knot was just out of his reach. He strained at the wire, trying to force it over his head. But it was too tight. He twisted his body to one side, wondering if he could roll off the metal bed. But even if he could get his legs and chest off the bed, that would still leave his head firmly fixed. It was hopeless.

Like a snared animal, he tore at the wire. Far away, the audience applauded again. He could feel madness creeping up on him. There was nobody in sight. There was no way he could free himself. It was only a matter of time.

"I'm sorry, ma'am. You can't go in there."

Linda Thorn found herself blocked by the man at the stage door, just as Nicholas had been. His colleague was also there, biting into a roast beef sandwich that he had just unwrapped. It had taken her more than twenty minutes to get there. Too long.

Now she stared resentfully at the two men. Had she been writing this, there wouldn't have been any security guards. But there they were—and she didn't know what to do. The show was sold out, so she couldn't even buy a ticket to get in. And where was Nicholas?

She smiled sweetly. "I'm looking for my nephew," she explained. "He's young . . . about fourteen. With dark hair and glasses."

The guard with the sandwich paused in mid-bite. "He was here," he said. "He was looking for a friend."

"Did you let him in?"

"No."

"We don't let anyone in unless they have a pass," the first guard said. "The last time I saw the kid, he was hanging around in the street. You'll probably find him outside."

"I didn't see him on the way in," Linda said.

"Well, look for him on the way out," the guard replied.

Meekly, Linda left the stage door area. She stopped beside the same poster that Nicholas had read. If the two guards really had been there all along, as seemed likely, then Nicholas wouldn't have been able to get in either. Linda looked at her watch. It was nearly three o'clock. According to the poster, the show was due to end at a quarter to four. Linda looked around for somewhere to sit down. She would just have to wait. It was a sunny afternoon. Maybe she'd get herself some coffee and a cookie.

"He's okay," she muttered to herself. "He probably got himself a ticket. Yeah, I bet right now he's just sitting back, enjoying the show."

Nicholas watched, helpless, as the third section of the stage began its downward journey. He had already seen the other two sections go up and down and had estimated that they took about forty seconds to reach the bottom. So in forty seconds he would die.

Rapidly it was getting closer . . . a massive bulk of blackness that stretched out like some sort of end-of-the-world, blotting out his vision. He couldn't move. He couldn't scream. He could only watch.

The gears engaged. The pipes stopped turning. And the stage jerked to a halt about twelve feet above him. For this part of the show it had been lowered only halfway. Nicholas could hardly control himself. Underneath the gag he wanted to laugh. He felt as if he were going mad.

But Nicholas didn't go mad. As the stage rose once again he forced himself to calm down. Closing his eyes, he thought of Jeremy. Jeremy needed him. He had to find him. Somehow he had to get away. If only he had the power . . . the power! He had already accepted that there was no way he could untie the wire or squeeze himself off the bed. But his mind was still free. He still had his power and that night, in Linda's apartment, he had used it in a new way. It had been stronger than ever. He couldn't reach Jeremy anymore—and even if he could, it would have been useless. But what of Linda? She had to be somewhere near. Could he somehow communicate with her?

From the day that he had discovered it, Nicholas had used his power only with Jeremy. He had never even considered whether it was possible to send his thoughts to anyone else. It had always been as if he were one end of a telephone line and Jeremy the other. But now he thought again. A telephone line could have more than one extension. He just had to concentrate.

It was difficult. First he had to damp down the very sense of excitement that the thought had given him. Then—more difficult still—he had to forget where he was, the fear that there might be only minutes left to him. Suddenly everything was very quiet. All the sections of the stage were still as the show approached its climax.

Nicholas closed his eyes and sent out a message for help.

Linda was sitting outside a health food shop on 52nd Street, a plastic cup of acorn coffee in one hand and a dried-fig cookie balanced on her knee. It was a sunny day and she had nothing else to do. She was certain that Nicholas would show up at any moment, perhaps with good news. She bit into the cookie, still warm from the oven.

"Linda . . ."

"Yes?"

The voice had come from close to her, just behind her head. Linda turned around, expecting to see Nicholas there. But the doorway was empty. She looked up and down the street, then shrugged. She must have imagined it. Her name hadn't been so much spoken as whispered, and if anyone had whispered in all the din of the traffic, she would never have heard it.

"Linda . . ."

But there it was again. And now she realized that the voice had come from inside her. It was impossible to describe. The voice was inside her head.

"Nicholas?" she quavered.

"Help me, Linda. Help!"

"Where are you, Nicholas? What's going on?"

The stream of pedestrians along 52nd Street was now making a wide arc on the sidewalk to avoid her. As far as they could see, Linda was holding a conversation with herself. But Linda ignored them. She couldn't even hear the traffic anymore.

"I'm under Radio City, Linda. Under the stage. Come quickly."

Dropping the cookie, Linda stood up. Once again she looked for Nicholas along the street, trying to convince herself that he was there. She knocked into a woman carrying a guidebook, spilling coffee. The woman hurried on, afraid. Under the stage? Nicholas certainly wasn't anywhere on the street.

"Hurry, Linda . . ."

Almost in a trance, Linda crossed the street and went back to the stage door. She didn't even try to understand what was happening. It was beyond her experience. All that mattered was to get into Radio City, to find her way under the stage. There would be time enough for explanations later.

There was only one guard at the stage door when she returned. She stopped in front of him, wondering what she was going to say.

"Look, ma'am," the guard began. "I told you . . ."

"Linda!"

She jerked the coffee cup, throwing the contents into the guard's face. The coffee wasn't hot enough to scald him, but it took him by surprise, momentarily blinding him. The guard shouted. But Linda had already seen the staircase to the right of the passageway. Spinning the plastic cup over her shoulder, she ran for it, disappearing before the guard could see where she had gone.

Linda ran down two flights of stairs and into a corridor. Now something even crazier was beginning to happen. It was as if she were suffering from double vision. She could see the corridor, the fire bucket, the sign pointing to the Musicians' Club Room. But at the same time she could make out pipes, valves, and strange stars made from metal girders that hovered like ghosts over the first image. She stumbled to a halt, thinking she was going to walk straight into a golden pillar that sprouted impossibly out of the floor. But the pillar wasn't there. It was close to wherever Nicholas was. Half of what she was seeing, she was seeing through his eyes.

She turned a corner, saw the camel, ran past it, and arrived at the stage control area. Now she could see the pipes and the valves clearly. Nicholas had to be here somewhere. She gazed down at the shadowy rectangle, but apart from the machinery, there was nothing there.

"In the corner, Linda. Come down to the corner."

There was something there, spread out on a metal support. Linda was startled by a loud buzzing, then a click. Across the floor, levers sprang to attention. She looked up. Part of the ceiling was lowering itself, a vast stretch of wood and metal running the full length of the rectangle.

"Hurry, Linda! Hurry! Hurry!"

Nicholas had heard the machinery activate itself. He opened

his eyes. The third section of the stage was moving down toward him an inch at a time. The pipes were turning. Once again the spreading darkness pressed down on him. He waited for it to stop as it had stopped before, halfway down. Larger and larger it loomed in his vision. Sweat trickled down the side of his head, dripping into the pool around his neck. The stage reached the midway point, but still it came. Now it was only ten feet away . . . ten seconds to go. Nicholas screamed without making any sound. His whole body was rigid, his hands clutching the edge of the metal bed. The wire cut into his mouth. The blackness was crushing him even before the stage reached him.

But then he felt someone tugging at the wire. He couldn't see who it was. He couldn't see anything. He was aware only of the massive bulk of the stage, six feet away, five feet away. . . . The wire came free. Hands gripped him. He was pulled off the bed and onto the floor. There was a muffled explosion in his ears as the stage came to rest on its support. If he had lifted a hand, he could have touched it. Now as he lay on the floor, it was only a few feet above him, the height of the metal bed. But he was alive. And Linda was holding him, cradling his head in her arms.

They stayed like that for what seemed an eternity, unable to stand up even if they had wanted to. Then at last the machinery connected and lifted the stage back up to join the other two sections at the top. Getting to her feet, Linda dragged Nicholas across the floor and propped him up against the wall.

"Thanks," Nicholas said. His voice was a whisper.

"Nicholas! What happened to you?"

Gently, Linda brushed the hair out of his eyes. He looked terrible. One of his eyes was blackened, his lips puffy and swollen. His whole body was drenched in sweat, and his arm, hanging out of the tatters of his shirt, was an ugly confusion of black, blue, and red. He looked like a rag doll that had just been put through a meat grinder.

"Worm . . ." Nicholas choked on the word and drew a deep breath. "It was him."

"He's half-killed you."

"Only half?" A ghost of a smile appeared on Nicholas's face. "I reached you."

"It was weird." Linda shook her head. "Like you were talking inside me."

"I've . . . never done it before." Nicholas fingered the cut on the side of his mouth. "My power—it's getting stronger."

Linda remembered the guard at the stage door and glanced nervously at the ladder leading out of the rectangle. "We've got to move," she said. "Can you walk?"

"I think so."

She reached out and helped Nicholas up. For a moment he swayed, unsure of himself. But now that the worst was over, he felt that his injuries weren't as bad as he had thought. Worm had beaten him, bruised him, and almost frightened him to death. But there were no broken bones. He could move all his fingers, and although he was physically exhausted, he could stand on his own two feet.

Even so, the ladder was an ordeal. Climbing Everest would have been about as easy. Nicholas went first, with Linda right behind him in case he fell. The machinery was silent now. The show had almost reached its end. He took the ladder one rung at a time, making sure of his grip before he pulled himself up onto the next one. He had never felt so tired. All he wanted to do was sleep.

Somehow he reached the top, then turned around to wait for Linda. As she climbed over the edge of the rectangle, he saw her face fall. Nicholas turned around. The security guard was standing there, his hair still wet from the coffee. There were another three men with him. One of them was a policeman, his holster unfastened, his hand hovering over his gun.

Linda straightened up and put a hand on Nicholas's shoulder.

"I don't know what you think you're doing," the security guard said. "But you're both under arrest."

= NINE =

The Golden Cup

NICHOLAS AND LINDA were escorted back to the stage door under close guard: one man in front of them, one behind them, and one on each side. But if their guards were afraid that they might try to escape, they needn't have worried. Nicholas could barely walk, leaning on Linda for support. For her part, Linda had tried to reason with the men . . . but without success. Both of them knew that it was only a matter of time before Nicholas was recognized. He had lost his glasses in the fight, and his sweat had mixed with the hair dye, blackening his collar and leaving light streaks in his hair. Nobody had commented on his bruises. From the way they were looking at Linda, they could have suspected that she was to blame.

They reached the stage door. A police car was parked in the street outside, the light on its roof still flashing. A second policeman stood beside it, holding the door open to receive the prisoners.

"Hold on a minute," Linda protested, digging in her heels. "We're not criminals. We haven't done anything wrong."

"You were trespassing," the policeman said.

"And you assaulted me," the security guard added. "With a cup of coffee."

"You don't understand . . ."

"You can tell us about it down at the precinct," the policeman said.

He nudged them toward the door. At that moment the

telephone rang. The security guard went into the glass booth to answer it. At the same time, the policeman tried to push Linda out onto the street. But still she resisted. Once Nicholas got inside the police station, she was certain that he would never leave.

"Yes, Mrs. Carnitt. We got them," the guard was saying.

"Come on," the policeman insisted.

"You're making a mistake," Linda pleaded.

Then the security guard reappeared, leaving the telephone receiver lying on his desk. He was frowning, puzzled. "You can let them go," he said.

"Let them go?" the policeman repeated.

"It's all right," the security guard explained. He was evidently as unhappy about it as the policeman. "We're not pressing any charges."

"What do you mean?" the policeman demanded.

"Mrs. Carnitt wants to see them," the security guard growled. "She's taking personal responsibility."

The name seemed to have a magical effect on the policeman. He loosened his grip on Linda and relaxed, almost smiling. "Mrs. Carnitt?" he said. "Well, I suppose that's all right then." He looked closely at Nicholas. "I'm sure I've seen you somewhere before," he muttered. "I should really run the two of you in anyway. But if Mrs. Carnitt is willing to take responsibility for you, that's your good luck." He adjusted the cap on his head and walked out to join his partner at the car.

"You'd better come with me," the security guard said.

They walked back to the elevator and the guard pressed the call button.

"Who is Mrs. Carnitt?" Nicholas asked.

"Only about the most powerful woman in New York," she said. "It was Mrs. Carnitt who produced the show that's here at the moment—*The Children of God*."

"She's a theater producer?"

"Not exactly. She runs a charity—the Golden Cup. It works exclusively with children . . . you know, hospitals for sick children, starving children in third world countries, prevention of cruelty to children, and that sort of thing. The charity's been around only about a year, but in that time she's raised millions. Only last week she was having dinner in the

White House. Last month she was on the cover of *Time* magazine. She's an amazing woman."

The elevator arrived and the three of them got in. The guard pressed a button for the third floor.

"So what does she want with us?" Nicholas asked as the doors slid shut.

"Heaven knows. But you'll notice that the cop wasn't prepared to argue with her. She works hand in hand with the police on things like drug abuse and delinquency. They say that she's—"

But then the doors opened and the guard ushered them out into a carpeted corridor lit by chandeliers. Nicholas and Linda followed him to a door a short way down. He knocked once.

"Come in!" a voice called out.

The guard opened the door. "They're here, Mrs. Carnitt," he said.

"Thank you, John. Are you all right?"

"I guess so, Mrs. Carnitt."

"Then you can leave us."

The guard stepped back, took one last look at Linda, and made his way back down the corridor. Linda glanced at Nicholas, and together they went in.

The door led into a large office furnished with old-fashioned chairs and sofas made of dark wood and lined with silk. One wall was given over to filing cabinets, another to books. Blue velvet curtains hung from ceiling to floor on each side of two windows that looked out onto Sixth Avenue. Everything in the room looked expensive: from the paintings on the wall and the cut-glass vase of flowers on the desk to the woman who sat facing them.

Mrs. Carnitt was one of the most extraordinary women he had ever seen. She was wearing a dress of vivid yellow and black, with a huge bow fastened at the neck. Tiny gold pellets hung in a cluster from her ears, matched by a gold bracelet on her wrist. Her hair was pitch black, pressed tight against her forehead but hanging loose at the back. Her eyes, too, were black—or such was the effect of her eye shadow, which was painted on so thickly that it made it difficult to see her pupils. Her eyelashes, thin and rather cruel, completed the effect. Against the general pallor of her skin, her makeup was almost demonic. Her bright red lips and fingernails could have been stained during a blood sacrifice.

This woman is evil, Nicholas thought. But then she smiled at him and gestured toward a high-backed chair and he remembered what Linda had told him. He sat down, regretting his first impression. But for her, he would have been on his way to prison.

"Are you all right?" she asked, looking at him anxiously.

"Yes, thanks." Nicholas nodded.

"And you, my dear." Mrs. Carnitt turned to Linda. "You attacked one of my security men. You were trespassing where you had no right to be. What do you have to say for yourself?"

Linda shrugged. "I was looking for him."

"It was kind of you to stop them," Nicholas broke in. "They were going to arrest us."

Mrs. Carnitt lifted a perfectly manicured hand. "I assumed that you were trying to break in to see the show," she said. "Sometimes the worst things are done for the best motives. How could I have anyone arrested when they were so eager to hear the Good Word?"

"Well, it wasn't quite like that," Linda admitted.

Mrs. Carnitt frowned. "Then tell me, my dear. What was it quite like?"

Linda looked at Nicholas. Nicholas hesitated, still unsure of the woman who sat in front of him. But Linda was less reticent. She had been working on her own for too long. Mrs. Carnitt could be a powerful friend.

So she told her story . . . the disappearance of Joe Fanelli, her research, the missing children. She explained how she had first met Nicholas, describing how his brother had been kidnapped. She even used their real names, names that brought a sharp glance from Mrs. Carnitt. Linda was gambling. If Mrs. Carnitt wanted them arrested, it was still within her power. But everything she had heard about the woman and her organization told her that she was on safe ground.

At last she finished. Mrs. Carnitt sat silently, deep in thought. Nicholas watched her, his eyes narrow, certain that Linda had gone too far. But then Mrs. Carnitt spoke.

"It's an extraordinary story," she said. "I wouldn't have believed it if I couldn't see part of the evidence with my own eyes." She pointed at Nicholas. "This man . . . Worm . . . he did all this to you?"

"Yes," Nicholas answered.

"What a monster!" Mrs. Carnitt shook her head. The golden earrings swayed and tinkled quietly. "And to a child! Sometimes I despair." She stood up. "But perhaps I can help you."

"How?" Nicholas asked.

"Do you know who I am?"

"Linda told me a little about you . . ." Nicholas began.

But Mrs. Carnitt had turned away, gazing out of the window over the endless bustle of New York.

"When I first came here," she said, "I was shocked. Everywhere I looked there was sin and depravity. Of course, all big cities have their share of vice. But New York . . . so grand, so splendid? How could it be that beneath all those glittering skyscrapers, symbols of man's achievement, so many people could choose to live in the gutter?

"I have no children of my own, but I was determined then and there to help the children of the world, starting with the children of America. Fortunately, I had money. I raised more money. I formed an organization which I called the Golden Cup. It is, if you like, an image of the Bible, the good book in which so many blessings are waiting to be poured forth."

She crossed to a bookshelf and took out a book which she laid on the desk. It was a Bible bound in cloth with a small golden cup emblazoned in the center.

"I am often accused of being naive," she continued, "but I am convinced that this one book contains all the answers to life's problems. The world is a sorry place. There are wars and there are famines. People choke in the pollution. Some have difficulty finding jobs and the money to feed their families, while at the same time vast amounts are wasted on nuclear weapons and other machines of destruction. Everywhere there is violence. Our books are violent. Our films are violent. But the Bible says, "Blessed are the peacemakers, for they are the children of God."

"That is the title of the show I have put on here. *The Children of God*. They are our hope for the future." She raised a finger. "And it is my determination that every child in America will one day, soon, own a Bible. That is what I am now working on. I hired Radio City, put on this show, to demonstrate that the Bible isn't just a dry, dusty piece of work. It lives. It can help us. "Every child shall have a Bible." That is the motto of the Golden Cup. And Nicholas, I want you to take this one. Read it. Enjoy it. Learn from it."

Nicholas picked up the Bible, feeling a little embarrassed. He was willing to believe that Mrs. Carnitt was everything that Linda had said she was. But she still hadn't answered his question.

"It's very kind of you, Mrs. Carnitt," he said. "I'll read it tonight. But how will it help me find Jeremy?"

Mrs. Carnitt smiled for a second time. "I was coming to that," she said. "I've described my work to give you an idea of the scope of my operation. I couldn't have gotten this far without help. The President of the United States himself was generous enough to donate ten thousand dollars to the Golden Cup. In my work I see hundreds of officials . . . at all levels. You already have experience of my influence with the police.

"I can make inquiries. You tell me that children with paranormal powers are disappearing. Personally, I don't believe in such powers." She held up a hand to forestall any argument. "Sometimes God sends us little miracles that we like to pretend have a human cause. The paranormal is only a scientific term for what cannot be explained, and I prefer faith to science.

"It is enough that Jeremy has been abducted and your uncle killed. I shall make some phone calls. The police, who have so far ignored your brother's plight will take a fresh interest. I have my contacts . . . in offices and on the street. Before you go, leave me a number and an address where I can reach you."

"We can't do that," Nicholas said.

"You don't trust me?"

Nicholas blushed, ashamed of himself. Linda cast a sharp glance in his direction. But Mrs. Carnitt was still smiling.

"If I wanted you arrested, I could do it now," she said. "But you seem an honest boy to me. I believe your story. I won't give your number to the police. But I'll be in touch soon. Perhaps with good news."

Linda opened her purse and took out a date book. She scribbled on a page, tore it out, and handed it to Mrs. Carnitt.

"You can reach me here," she said. "If we're not in, there's an answering machine."

"I'll do what I can," Mrs. Carnitt promised. "And in the meantime, young man, I'd do something about that disguise of yours. I recognized you the moment you came in. If you're not careful, someone else will too."

= TEN =

Nightfall in New York

THEY TOOK A taxi back to the apartment. Nicholas was too tired to walk, too tired even to speak. He gazed out of the window as they drove past the skyscrapers, joining the long lines of cars and buses on the way home.

There was the Citadel, glowing a dark red in the last rays of the setting sun. In the distance were the glistening waters of the East River with a cable car from the Roosevelt Island Tramway station crawling along the steel wire high above, on its way to the island. There was Central Park, already beginning to empty as the shadows crept in.

Nicholas hardly took in anything he saw—and yet he was aware of something . . . something they had passed. He didn't know what it was, but somewhere inside him he knew it was important. Central Park? The river? He shook his head, forgetting it. Whatever it was, it could wait.

But he was still deep in thought as they climbed the stairs to Linda's apartment.

"What's up?" Linda asked, untangling her keys.

"Mrs. Carnitt . . ." Nicholas began.

"You don't trust her?" Linda turned the first lock. "She's about the best chance we have of finding Jeremy."

"How do we know she won't give this number to the police?"

"Well, if she's done that, they'll be here now."

But the apartment was empty. While Linda prepared a meal, Nicholas stripped off his clothes and relaxed in a steaming bath. His body was not a pretty sight after the mauling it had received at Worm's hands, but the hot water seemed to draw out most of the pain, and by the time he was toweling himself dry, he felt almost completely recovered.

He went back into the living room swathed in a towel, his hair still dripping. Linda handed him a bathrobe. "Wear this," she said. "It's probably too big, but you can't eat dressed like that."

"Is it yours?" Nicholas asked.

"No. A boyfriend of mine left it here."

"Where is he now?"

Linda sighed. "I don't know. He didn't like my cooking."

"And what have you cooked tonight?"

"Buckwheat pancakes stuffed with cabbage and banana."

"Wonderful."

In fact, it tasted better than it sounded, and to his surprise Nicholas managed to eat his way through three helpings. When they had finished, Linda stacked the plates in the sink and poured two glasses of apple juice. It was quiet outside now. Only the occasional howl of a police car reminded them that New York never really slept.

"There is one thing Mrs. Carnitt doesn't know," Nicholas said, sipping his juice.

"What's that?" Linda asked.

"I overheard something in Radio City just before Worm grabbed me. He was talking with a man with a Spanish accent. It didn't make much sense. . . ."

"Tell me," Linda said.

So Nicholas repeated the conversation—or as much of it as he could remember. Some phrases came easily to mind: "Ninety-five percent pure . . ." ". . . the last shipment . . ." He remembered also the location, Fulton, and the time, one o'clock the following night. It was only the weight that confused him. He was sure that the men had mentioned eighty kilos, but Linda stopped him.

"That's impossible," she said. "It must have been eight kilos."

"I'm sure it was eighty," Nicholas protested. "Eighty kilos, ninety-five percent pure . . . that's what they said. But I don't know what they were talking about. Do you?"

"I think so," Linda said. "I wish I didn't, but I think I do."

She got up and searched through a pile of papers on the floor, eventually pulling out a thick file. She put it on the table, then poured two more glasses of juice.

"Drugs," she said.

"Drugs?"

"Cocaine . . . heroin . . . something like that. It makes sense, Nicholas. My novel, *A Deadly Day in June*, it was all about drug smuggling, and I spent a few months this year doing research."

She opened the file.

"I don't know much about it, but everything you heard makes sense only if you're talking about heroin. The purity—it has to be refined. The security—well, that's obvious. Even the route. Back in the sixties most of the heroin in New York came from Montreal. There's about a thousand miles of border between Canada and America and only a couple of hundred border guards. It used to be the main smuggling route. It's just the weight. Eighty kilograms!"

"What's wrong?"

"It would be worth millions and millions of dollars. If this was just one shipment, well, Nicholas, it would seem that you were spying on just about the biggest smuggling operation in the history of America."

"It *was* eighty kilograms," Nicholas protested. He scratched his head.

"What's wrong?" Linda asked.

"I just don't get it," Nicholas said. "If Worm is involved in drug smuggling, well, that's fair enough. I mean, I wouldn't put anything past him. But where does Jeremy come into it? Or me, for that matter? We've got nothing to do with drugs."

"If it was eight kilograms . . ." Linda began.

"But it wasn't."

The two of them sat in silence.

"Joe Fanelli," Linda muttered at last. "He was found pumped full of drugs. There's a link for you."

"But why?"

"Kids with paranormal powers being kidnapped. A massive drug smuggling operation." Linda shook her head. "It's crazy."

"Unless it wasn't drugs. They could have been talking about something else."

Linda closed the file. "We're not going to get anywhere talking about it tonight," she said. "You ought to get some sleep. But tomorrow we'll go and see a man."

"Who?" Nicholas asked.

"His name is Bob Young. He's with the FBI Special Drugs Division."

"How do you know him?"

"I was introduced to him when I was doing my research. I knew him for a while. In fact, I couldn't have written my book without him. He's a strange sort of guy, but helpful. And he knows what he's talking about."

Nicholas yawned. "You're right," he said. "I'm tired. But I still don't see the connection."

"Maybe it'll be clearer in the morning."

"Maybe."

Linda carried the glasses over to the sink, then, ignoring his protests, she straightened the sheets and blankets on the couch for Nicholas. Finally she kissed him lightly on the cheek.

"Good night, Nicholas," she said. "Don't worry about it. Just try to sleep."

Nicholas hung the bathrobe over the back of a chair and curled up under the blankets. As he lay back, the events of the day seemed to rush in on him. His eyes felt heavy. He could have fallen asleep then and there. But he forced himself to stay awake. Lying in the darkness, he concentrated as he had every night in Linda's apartment, sending his thoughts out of his body. The sensation was familiar to him now, the separation of mind and body. And every time he did it, it was a little easier.

Once again he flew over the shadowy configuration of New York, searching in the darkness for some sign of his brother. He would have been grateful for anything: a cry for help, a whisper of his name. Even Jeremy's heartbeat would have been enough of a signal.

But there was nothing. If anything, the chasm between them had grown. He was alone in an immense void. It was as if his brother had ceased to exist.

* * *

Mr. Banes walked down the whitewashed corridor, the heels of his shoes rapping on the tiled floor. He was carrying a plastic tray. On the tray was a sandwich, a pitcher of milk, and an apple. A guard, sitting on a chair outside a plain wooden door, stood to attention and produced a ring of keys. Motioning him to wait, Mr. Banes balanced the tray on his knee and adjusted his hearing aid, turning the volume up. The boy had been in the Treatment Center all day. His voice would be weak.

Smiling to himself, Mr. Banes nodded at the guard, who selected a key, inserted it into the lock, and turned it. The tumblers fell with a metallic rattle. The guard pushed the door open and stood well back, allowing Mr. Banes to pass. There was something about the man who was master of the island that made you want to shrink away from him.

"You can leave the door unlocked," Mr. Banes said.

"Yes, sir, Mr. Banes," the guard muttered.

Mr. Banes looked at the guard, two sparks of good humor dancing behind the circles of glass. "The boy is our guest," he explained. "Not our prisoner."

The door opened into a small, square room. A bunk ran along one wall with a bare plastic table and a chair opposite. There was only one window, barred and too high up to look through. The room was lit by a naked light bulb behind a wire grill, controlled from outside. The walls, the floor, and the ceiling were covered with a leathery white material, cushioned against the brickwork. Mr. Banes might have described it as a guest room. Anyone else would have called it a padded cell.

Mr. Banes set the tray down on the table and pulled back the chair. Then he sat down and took out a cigarette—black with a single gold band around the filter. When he lit it, it smelled of burning hair. He sat in silence for a minute, his eyes fixed on the figure that lay hunched up on the bunk. Again the smile flickered on his lips. He leaned back and blew a perfect smoke ring that hung black in the air before dissolving into an ugly cloud.

Jeremy had been on the island for only four days, but in that time he had changed. His hair had been cut short and he had lost weight. There were dark hollows in his cheeks and the prison uniform—blue jeans and a denim shirt with his number, 300, stenciled in black ink on his breast pocket—hung off him clumsily. There was a plaster on his forehead. His eyes, when he opened them, were bleak and distant.

"I've brought you some food, Jeremy," Mr. Banes said, blowing another smoke ring.

Jeremy said nothing.

"You have to get strong," Mr. Banes continued. He stood up, carrying the sandwich over to the bunk. "Eat this. It's good."

As Mr. Banes approached, Jeremy drew himself up on the bunk, huddling in the corner with his knees under his chin.

"You don't have to be afraid of me, Jeremy," Mr. Banes went on in the same kindly voice. "I'm your friend. I want to look after you. I have great plans for you, Jeremy. You're almost one of us now. You're going to make us all proud of you."

Jeremy stared at Mr. Banes with wide, haunted eyes. For a moment he was back in the mirrored room, strapped to the chair, his eyes forced open, the leather band in his mouth and the wires trailing from his head. Mr. Banes had been there, leaning over him, probing, pushing, pressing the buttons that brought the pain. How could he be his friend?

But had it been Mr. Banes? Jeremy was confused, the memory of those terrible hours already a jumble in his mind. Somebody had hurt him. But Mr. Banes was bringing him food. He was speaking gently to him. Then who . . . ?

"Nicholas," he whispered in a voice so low that even with his hearing aid at full volume Mr. Banes barely caught the word.

"Nicholas?" he repeated. "Jeremy, my dear boy. Nicholas is to blame for all this. He was the one who hurt you. Don't you remember?"

Jeremy closed his eyes, aware of a fresh stab of pain that he couldn't understand.

"Nicholas betrayed you," the soft voice continued. "You helped him get away. He was on the wall. But when they came for you, did he try to stop them? No. He left you to them. He just watched as they took you and then saved his own skin."

Yes. It had happened like that. Jeremy went back in his mind, back to the wall outside the Comedy Theatre. He had lifted Nicholas onto the wall just before the three men caught up with him. And now he could see his brother, his hair blowing in the wind, a great smile on his face, pointing down, mocking him. And he could hear his laughter, loud and shrill, ringing in his ears. Nicholas had planned it from the very start. He had led his brother into a trap and left him to suffer the consequences.

"Nicholas hated you," Mr. Banes said. "They all hated you . . . your Uncle Don, the kids at school . . . even your so-called friends in England. And do you know why they hated you, Jeremy? It was because of your power, the power that I have discovered in you. You were different from them and they were afraid of you. And because they were afraid of you, they hated you. It's always the same. All the great men in history have been envied and despised. And you will be a great man, Jeremy. We will see to that."

Jeremy looked at Mr. Banes and suddenly he felt a surge of gratitude and affection so strong that it brought tears to his eyes. He had got it wrong before. Mr. Banes had never hurt him. Mr. Banes was his friend. And what he said was true. In all his life he had never had a friend. Not until he came to the island.

"Please, sir," he said. "What's going to happen to me?"

Mr. Banes flicked ash into a corner of the food tray. A few gray specks floated on the surface of the milk. "There will have to be more treatments," he said.

Jeremy shuddered.

"It's for your own good, Jeremy. We have to help you see things our way. It's the only way to make you strong."

"Yes, sir."

"And then, when we think you are ready, we will allow you to join us. One day, soon, Jeremy, we will rule the world—and you will serve us for the rest of your life. And if you serve us well, perhaps we will allow you to kill your brother, Nicholas. You'd like that, wouldn't you?"

Jeremy thought about it. Once again he saw Nicholas, perched on the wall, pointing down, laughing at him.

"Yes, sir," he said. "I'd like that very much."

At last Nicholas slept. And dreamed.

He was on a rocky outcrop, perched on the edge of a beach

beside a great sea. The waves were rolling far beneath him, endlessly crashing forward as if struggling toward a point they would never reach. A pale moon hung in the sky, reflected in the sea. A cold breeze blew over the water, whipping up the surf and racing across the sand, which swirled around like a dog chasing its tail. Three figures stood on the beach, too far away for him to be able to see their faces. But he felt that they were looking at him.

There was a movement behind him and he turned around. There was another boy standing beside him, a boy of his own age and height. Nicholas had been afraid, alone on the rock, but seeing the other boy, he felt comforted. He knew that he had seen him somewhere before. And even without speaking he knew that he was a friend.

"Who are you?" he asked.

"Martin Hopkins," the boy said.

"Martin . . ." Nicholas smiled. "I saw your name in a newspaper."

"Yes. But that was at another time, in another place."

The waves pounded against the rock. They seemed to be getting nearer. At the same time, the wind blew in faster, sharper gusts. Somewhere behind the horizon, underneath the soft glow of the moon, something was taking shape. Nicholas pulled his jacket around him, shivering.

"We haven't got much time," Martin Hopkins said. "Listen to me, Nicholas. You are one of the five. So is your brother."

"Jeremy . . ."

"He's suffered. So will you. But you can't give in. We are the only thing that stands between the world and the Old Ones."

"Who are the Old Ones?"

"They ruled at the beginning of time, when all was dark. They are the creatures of darkness. And now they've come back. They mean to destroy you."

"Why?"

"Five defeated them once and five shall rise up against them again. That's the prophecy. But there have to be five. If one falls, we all fall. Only together do we have the power to defeat them."

"What can I do?"

"Find your brother . . . if he is still your brother. He's in their hands. Who can say what they'll have done to him."

"But . . . down there . . . on the beach." Nicholas pointed at the three unmoving figures. Together with Martin and himself, that made five. So Jeremy had to be among them.

But Martin shook his head. "This is another time, another place. Find your brother, Nicholas. And then find me."

"Wait!"

The storm, when it broke, was so violent, so sudden, that Nicholas was deafened. Thunder exploded all around him. The ground trembled. The whole sky disintegrated. The wind roared. For a moment everything was white, everything except for a huge shape looming over the horizon, vaguely human, its arms stretching out toward him. Nicholas fell to his knees. And then the sea rose up, the waves black and furious, towering above him. Slowly, they curved around, then smashed down on him.

And then he was sitting up on the couch in Linda's room, the sweat on his face and chest cold in the cool night breeze. The lights were on and Linda was standing by the doorway, half-wrapped in a bathrobe.

"What is it?" she said. "You were shouting . . ."

Nicholas took a deep breath and pulled the blanket back up to his neck.

"It was nothing," he said. "Just a bad dream."

= ELEVEN =

Horse and Boy

GETTING THROUGH TO Special Agent Bob Young was not as easy as Linda had thought it would be. She called the number he had given her at their last meeting, but at first his office denied all knowledge of him. It was only when she said that she had important information for him that they passed her through to a man who called himself Mr. Smith. "An alias, no doubt," Linda muttered. Mr. Smith was hardly more helpful. Mr. Young was away at the moment, he said: Could he perhaps be of assistance? Finally, after a conversation that had grown gradually more heated, Linda had declared that she would tell only Bob Young himself what she knew. She demanded to meet him face to face. Mr. Smith said he would call her back. He did so twenty minutes later. Mr. Young would meet her, he said, but only at a time and at a place chosen by himself.

The time was one o'clock. The place was the top of the World Trade Center.

Now Linda and Nicholas stood a quarter of a mile up in the sky at the top of one of the tallest buildings in the world.

Linda was perplexed. "Why do we have to meet up here?" she grumbled. "Why not just in his office?"

"Maybe he likes the view," Nicholas suggested.

Despite himself, he had to admit that the view was spectacular. The streets and skyscrapers of Manhattan stretched away to the very horizon, disappearing at last in a soft gray haze. Everywhere he looked there was glass and steel: green, brown, white, black, and silver, like some bizarre crystal formation growing in a subterranean cave.

While Nicholas gazed over the railing, Linda walked around the bright blue metal catwalk that followed the four sides of the tower. As usual, the observation platform was crowded with tourists taking photographs of each other against the backdrop, as thousands had before them. More and more people were appearing, carried up by the escalator from the restaurants and souvenir shops on the floor below. But there was no sign of Bob Young. Linda looked at her watch. Ten past one. He was late.

She rejoined Nicholas and they stood together, their backs toward the city. Warm and mild 107 floors down, it was cold and blustery up here. Linda pulled her sweater around her shoulders. But Nicholas didn't seem to notice the cold.

"What's on your mind?" Linda asked.

"Jeremy." Nicholas spoke slowly, deliberately. "I know who's got him. And I know why. I even know where he is."

"What are you talking about?"

"Have you ever heard of the Old Ones?" Nicholas asked.

Linda shook her head.

"They're creatures . . . devils, I suppose. They took Jeremy because they're afraid of him. He has the power to stop them."

"To stop them doing what?"

"Taking over the world."

Now Linda was worried. "Do you want to go inside?" she said. "Maybe you'd better sit down for a few minutes."

"I'm not crazy." Nicholas smiled. "Although it must sound like it. It was in the dream I had last night, only now I'm not so sure it was a dream."

"And you saw Jeremy in the dream?"

"No. That was before. I saw something yesterday, in New York, something important. When I saw it, I knew that I'd found Jeremy." He sighed. "But I can't remember what it was. I just—"

"Linda?"

They were interrupted by a tall, well-built man who would have been handsome but for his shabby clothes and the three days growth of beard on his chin. His graying hair was long and unbrushed, his hands and face covered with grime. Nicholas guessed that he must be in his late thirties. Despite his general appearance, his eyes were bright and alert.

Linda squinted at him. "Bob . . . ?" she muttered. "Bob Young?"

"You wanted to see me," the man said.

"We've been waiting fifteen minutes for you."

"I've been here all along." The man looked around. "I had to be sure you weren't followed. Shall we go inside? I could do with something to eat."

Together they went back down to the restaurant and lined up at the self-service counter. Linda chose a salad for herself, and Nicholas halfheartedly ordered the same, sighing to himself as Bob opted for a cheeseburger, french fries, and a strawberry milk shake. As he carried the meal to a table, Bob smiled at Linda. "Yes, I know," he said. "Lots of saturated fat, carbohydrates, and calories, and not enough vitamins. And I still smoke."

"You're crazy," Linda muttered.

"Yeah . . . and hungry."

For a while they ate in silence. Linda had introduced Nicholas as her nephew, but had said no more. When he had finished, Bob sat back contentedly and lit a cigarette. An elderly tourist at the next table sniffed at his crumpled clothes and moved to another chair.

"How's the book going, Linda?" he asked at last.

"It's gone."

"You've still got my bathrobe?"

Linda glanced at Nicholas and blushed. "What are you doing, Bob?" she asked, hastily changing the subject. "Those awful clothes . . . and you stink! Your office said you were on vacation."

"It's a stakeout," Bob replied, lowering his voice. "Routine stuff. What did you want to see me for?"

"We need your help."

"Go on."

Linda repeated what Nicholas had overheard the day before in Radio City. She made no mention of Jeremy or the missing children. Bob would never have believed her, and anyway, it didn't seem relevant. She did, however, describe Nicholas's fight with Worm and his narrow escape under the stage. Bob could see the proof of it for himself. Nicholas's mouth was still bruised, one eye a dark shade of purple.

Bob listened without speaking. He frowned occasionally and once, when Linda mentioned "Fulton," he shook his head. When she had finished, he turned to Nicholas.

"You're involved in all this?" he asked.

"I'm afraid so," Nicholas said.

He looked at Linda. "So it's not just another of your crazy plots?"

"It's the truth, Bob," Linda said.

Bob drummed his fingertips on the table. "All right," he said. He turned back to Nicholas. "Let me tell you a bit about my work. It'll put things in perspective, and it'll tell you why you must have misheard that conversation."

Nicholas made as if to protest, but Bob raised a hand.

"Linda's probably told you," he began, "that I work for the FBI—Special Drugs Division. You probably think I'm some sort of spy, but most of my work is pretty routine. Only sometimes I have to go out on the street dressed like this, keeping an eye open for new developments.

"Now, you're telling me you've stumbled onto some sort of major drug ring. Heroin smugglers. I wonder how much you know about scag?"

"Scag?"

"It's one of the street names for heroin. There are plenty of them . . . antifreeze, jee gee, Mrs. White. Peanut butter. Helen. Horse and boy. But whatever you call it, there's no bigger threat to the security of this country. You know, people are scared of nuclear weapons and stuff like that. But heroin is a much bigger danger. It's like a sort of medieval plague . . . a killer.

"You think I'm exaggerating? Let me give you a few facts. There are about five hundred thousand heroin addicts in the United States alone. Nearly two hundred thousand of them are right here in New York. Have you ever walked through the Lower East Side alone at night? Don't. It's a hellhole. You'll find the scum of the earth hanging out there.

"When I talk of addicts, I'm talking about people who are more dead than alive. Maybe they did it for fun the first time. Now they can't function without it. It's like they'll go mad. They'd murder their own mother for another fix. Their veins have all collapsed. They're riddled with disease. The living dead.

"It's a huge market, Nicholas. Huge. You say you overheard people planning to smuggle in eighty kilos. Maybe that's worth around five million dollars on the street."

Nicholas whistled. "Five million?"

"Sure. Once it's been cut—which is to say, mixed—with quinine, glucose . . . maybe chalk and talcum powder too. Most street heroin is about six and one-half percent pure. You were talking ninety-five percent pure—so you can multiply the profits by fifteen just for starters. And believe me, five million dollars is just a drop in the ocean.

"Do you know how much heroin is smuggled into the United States every year? Of course, nobody knows for sure, but it's estimated at around one hundred billion dollars a year. Can you imagine that, Nicholas? I'm talking about a dollar sign and a one followed by eleven zeros."

Bob ran a hand through his hair.

"Heroin kills," he said. "Even as we sit here talking, it's killing someone . . . a lonely, dirty death."

There was a long silence.

"You said I must have misheard the conversation," Nicholas said at last.

"Sure." Bob stubbed out his cigarette. "It doesn't add up, and I'll tell you why. About a year ago we noticed something strange. There was suddenly less heroin around. Nobody knew why. It was as if someone were buying it all at source and storing it up—though that's impossible. You'd need too much money. But whatever the reason, there hasn't been a single shipment as big as the one you describe for ages. At least, not one that we've heard about.

"But the other thing is the route. You say it had come from Montreal and was going to "Fulton." Okay. The Fulton Fish Market is on the river, so heroin could come in there from the sea. You know . . . a small boat could meet a bigger one under cover of darkness and bring it into the city like that. But to carry it from Montreal to the Fulton Fish Market doesn't make any sense at all. It's in one door and out another. Where would it go from the fish market?"

"You said they'd have to cut it."

"Sure. But they'd do that on the Lower East Side, or

perhaps in Harlem. All you need is a big table, scales, plastic bags, and a few workers to help you along. A family could do it. They often do. Don't you see? If it was heroin your two conspirators were talking about, and there's no proof of that, they'd have no reason to take it to Fulton. None."

"Bob. We're not making this up," Linda said.

Bob shook his head. "I'm not saying you are. I just think that Nicholas didn't hear them properly. If they tried to kill him, that's another thing altogether. Why haven't you been to the police?"

Nicholas lowered his eyes. "I can't do that."

"Okay. I won't ask. But if you want my advice, you'll forget all about it. Get out of New York. Why don't you go back to Houston with Linda?"

"So you're not going to help us," Linda said.

"I can't help you. I'm sorry. My department's tied up in a delicate operation right now. I can't send my men on some wild goose chase. But believe me, if I thought there were anything in what you said . . ."

"Forget it," Linda muttered.

Bob stood up. "I still hope to buy a copy of *A Deadly Day in April* sometime," he said.

"It's *A Deadly Day in June*."

"Keep at it. And call me again if anything comes up. It was good to see you again, Linda. And good meeting you, Nicholas."

"Sure."

Ten minutes later Linda and Nicholas left, taking the elevator back down to the ground floor. Together they crossed the wide courtyard outside the World Trade Center, went down a flight of steps, and made their way to the nearest subway station. Neither of them saw a figure step out from behind a large circular fountain. The figure watched them until they had disappeared, then walked over to a telephone booth.

Bob Young fed a coin into the slot and began to dial a number.

= TWELVE =

Dead Fish

THERE WAS ONLY one button in the express elevator of the Citadel, and that wouldn't operate until a security pass had been slid into a narrow slot just below it. Once activated, the elevator sped directly to the top, traveling the ninety-two floors in less than a minute. It was lined on all four sides with dark mirrors, reflecting the man who stood wiping his palms against his trousers. At the last moment the elevator slowed down. The doors slid open and Mr. Banes stepped out.

He found himself in a short corridor that he knew well. Its walls were covered with a plain gray material. He was facing a set of double doors directly opposite the elevator—the only doors on the floor. Two black ebony statues flanked the doors. They were panthers, one snarling, one clawing at the air, both regarding the visitor with hostile eyes.

Mr. Banes paused between them. He lifted a hand and knocked. Then, with one last hasty wipe of his palms, he opened the doors and went in.

It was a huge room, dominated by a sweeping window that seemed to be perched on the edge of the world. The window was like a fabulous living painting. The sun was setting, a dark red with cubes of light from the skyscrapers below forming ever-changing patterns as offices were closed for the night. An airplane departing from Kennedy Airport inched its way across, a glittering silver arrow.

There was a figure shrouded in shadow sitting behind a desk. A spotlight in the ceiling shone down at Mr. Banes, blinding him as he stood rigid and silent. In a strange way he was glad that he could not see who spoke.

"Mr. Banes . . . I am dissatisfied." The voice was as hard and unforgiving as ever. "Worm failed to kill the boy in Radio City. It is possible that he overheard details of our operation."

Mr. Banes said nothing.

"He has associated himself with a woman who has also been taking an interest in our affairs. This must stop. How is the brother progressing?"

"He is a difficult subject." The words had come out dry and cracked. Mr. Banes cleared his throat and began again. "He is difficult. It's incredible, after all he's been through. Any ordinary boy—"

"But Jeremy Helsey is not ordinary!" the voice cut in, suddenly shrill. "Do you understand nothing? His power is . . . unimaginable."

"We are very close." Mr. Banes took a deep breath. "An ordinary child would have died by now—or been driven insane. We have broken down most of his resistance. He's begun to accept us as his friends. One more session . . ."

"I will supervise it personally. Tonight. In the meantime, Worm is prepared for our business?"

"Good. This is the last shipment. In just four days time we'll be ready to move. I cannot allow mistakes at this late stage. Tonight the Riders will be there."

"I understand."

The figure behind the desk leaned forward. For a moment it resembled a gigantic toad crouched before the leap.

"The woman need not concern us, Mr. Banes. Without the boy she'll be dismissed as a harmless crank. But Nicholas Helsey has become a problem. It's time he was put out of action."

"What do you want me to do?"

"Go back to the island and prepare Jeremy for tonight's session. And don't worry about young Nicholas. I will take care of him myself."

"Are you sure this is a good idea?" Linda asked.

"No," Nicholas replied. "But I can't think of a better one."

"How about going home and forgetting all about it?"

"Shhh!"

It was a quarter to one at the Fulton Fish Market near the southernmost edge of Manhattan. Nicholas and Linda had been there for half an hour, squatting behind a pile of crates which were separated from the East River by a wide, muddy avenue. To their left, the great causeway of the Brooklyn Bridge jutted out over the still water, suspended by a hundred slender cables from two arched towers. Overhead, a second road ran parallel to the river, supported about twenty feet above the ground on a series of thick pillars. The traffic was still coursing along both the road and the bridge, but little noise reached the Fulton Fish Market, which seemed to exist in a sunken, stinking world of its own.

Dead fish. Everything stank of it: the puddles, the grimy brickwork, the piles of rubble, the very air itself. The Fulton Fish Market existed only for fish. Across the avenue, opposite the crates where Nicholas and Linda were waiting, were the warehouses where tons of fish would be weighed and crated once the catch had been brought in from the East River. Behind them stood a line of attached pink and white buildings, five stories high. These were the offices of a dozen different companies: Smitty's Fillet House, La Roca Fish Co. Inc., East Bay Fish Company—the names painted on wooden awnings or on the bricks of the buildings themselves.

It was a cold and moonless night. The Fulton Fish Market was deserted. Nicholas and Linda were alone.

But now someone else was approaching. Nicholas grabbed hold of Linda and pulled her down behind the crates. It was a man dressed in jeans, an open-neck shirt, and a down vest. He had come from the Brooklyn Bridge end, keeping in the shadows of the overhead road and making as little noise as possible.

"Is it Worm?" Linda whispered.

"I don't know." Nicholas couldn't see the man's face. There was too little light. "I don't think so. He's too tall."

"Have you seen him before?"

"No."

Whoever he was, the man was making every effort not to be seen. He followed the shadows as far as the first warehouse and stopped, cocking an ear for any sound. There was a garbage truck parked in the street, dark green and dusty, its back hanging down like a pig's head with its open mouth gaping hungrily at the ground. The man concealed himself behind it, only his feet visible beneath the truck.

"What do you think?" Linda asked.

"Wait!" Nicholas hissed.

It was exactly one o'clock. Somewhere a bell struck. At the same moment, two cars approached from opposite ends of the thoroughfare. One was a black limousine, twice as long as an ordinary car, with smoked glass windows. It drove right past Nicholas and Linda and stopped near the entrance to the warehouse. The other car stopped, facing it. The doors opened and three men got out. They stood waiting while two men got out of the limousine. Nicholas tightened his hold on Linda's arm. One of the two men was Worm.

His companion was carrying a bag which was something between a large attaché case and a small suitcase. It was hard to see in the darkness, but Nicholas felt sure he knew him. On the wall. Three men running toward them. One raising a gun. Striking his brother down. This was the man.

The five of them stood without speaking, then turned and walked away together past the garbage truck and into the warehouse. A few seconds later there was a flicker of light as the inside of the building was illuminated. At the same time, the man they had spotted earlier left his hiding place behind the truck to join the others.

Nicholas straightened up.

"What are you doing?" Linda whispered.

"We won't learn anything over here," Nicholas replied.

"But . . ." Linda sighed as Nicholas sprinted across the street, then went after him. Together they concealed themselves in the shadows of the doorway and peered in.

The warehouse was long and narrow, with a stone floor glistening beneath the neon lights. Scales, buckets, signs, and chains hung in a confusion from the corrugated iron ceiling. Wire-mesh fences divided the place into sections, each one with its own metal table for the fish.

The five men had assembled at the end in two groups, keeping the distance between them. There was no sign of the mysterious spy. Nicholas and Linda watched from the door, afraid to go any farther. The men were talking, their voices low. One of them—a South American—had been carrying a briefcase, which he now opened. Worm stepped forward and took something out: a plastic bag filled with white powder. He walked back to his companion, tore it open, and pushed a fat finger in. Then he licked the finger.

"You are satisfied?" the South American asked.

Worm nodded.

"And you have the money?"

"I have the money."

The man smiled regretfully. "I am sad that this is to be our last . . . transaction, señor," he said. He clasped his hands together, acting for all the world like a salesman in a smart department store. "We have done much good business. But if you wish to change your mind, I can provide you with—"

"This is the last time," Worm interrupted. "The very last."

There was something about the way Worm spoke that made Nicholas narrow his eyes, but the South American simply shrugged.

"Then, the money . . ." he said.

Worm nodded at his companion, who set his own briefcase down on one of the metal tables and opened it, the lid masking its contents from the South American. Slowly, he reached inside.

"I presume you want to count it," Worm said.

At the door Linda stiffened, her mouth opening.

There was no money in the briefcase.

She had seen it a moment before the South American. A machine-gun: short and snub-nosed. The man cradled it in his arms as he brought the muzzle up over the lid and around to bear on the three dealers. The South American moved quickly, his hand scrabbling for the inside of his jacket. But not quickly enough. Worm's companion jerked at the trigger. The gun made hardly any sound . . . no more than a soft, deadly coughing. The South American seemed to throw himself—impossibly—into the air, his shoulder striking one of the buckets. Behind him, the other two suppliers spun in a crazy dance. The machine-gun stopped. The two men collided into each other and slumped to the floor. The bucket swung above them.

Linda managed to stifle the scream at the last moment.

What had begun as an adventure had become a nightmare, and she knew that if they were discovered, they were finished. Beside her, Nicholas had gone pale. Even above the rotting fish, the smell of cordite hung in the air. The South American groaned and rolled over. For a second all eyes were on him. Nicholas seized the opportunity to step back out of the doorway and into the darkness, pulling Linda with him.

"What . . . ?" Linda was too shocked to speak.

"Let's move!" Nicholas whispered.

But it was too late to run for cover. A speedboat heading down the East River had moored at the dock behind the warehouse. Now a powerful beam of light cut through the shadows as three more men ran over the concrete toward the door. There were two barrels to one side of the entrance. It was as much as Nicholas and Linda could do to throw themselves behind them before the other men arrived.

"All okay?"

"Sure. See to the bodies."

"The merchandise?"

"Here."

There was a grunt and a scuffle—a dead body being pulled along the floor. Then one of the men reappeared, the South American lying limp across his shoulders. Everything had been planned in advance. The man didn't hesitate. Carrying the body, he went over to the garbage truck and hauled it into the back. Then, while the other two corpses were similarly dealt with, he opened the cab door, stepped in, and started the engine. A moment later the garbage truck rumbled away, the glow of its taillamps fading in the darkness. Despite everything, Nicholas couldn't help feeling that the three drug dealers had met a fitting end.

Worm and his companion were the last to leave the warehouse. They paused in the doorway and for a moment their legs were only inches away from the barrels where Nicholas and Linda crouched, scarcely daring to breathe. Light, spilling out of the door, came so close to them that clinging to Linda, Nicholas could read the time on his watch. It was a quarter past one. He was astonished that as much as fifteen minutes had passed.

The two men walked past the barrels, Worm holding the

"merchandise," the other still carrying the case with the machine-gun.

"The last time," Worm repeated. He giggled, a high-pitched sound like a whimpering dog. "A shame it wasn't always so cheap."

The two men continued toward the point where the boat was moored, waiting to take them . . . where? Nicholas remembered what the special agent, Bob Young, had told them. Drugs might come into the Fulton Fish Market by boat, but not out. So where was Worm taking them? Once again he tried to recall what he had seen on the way from Radio City. He had only glanced at it out of the corner of his eye. But he had known it was important.

Carefully, he peered over the top of the barrel, hoping at least to see which direction the boat took. He made no sound, and afterward Linda would swear that she hadn't moved. Perhaps it was a cat . . . or a rat. They would never know. But there was a sound. Worm heard it. He stopped dead in his tracks and spun around. Nicholas watched wide-eyed as his companion fumbled with the case, opening it to take out the gun. But then Worm slapped a hand against his arm, stopping him. He squinted at the barrels through the darkness.

"Who is it?" he called out in a strange, singsong voice. "Spies is it?"

The two men began to walk back toward them. Nicholas looked at Linda. Her eyes darted past him. The two men were only twenty yards away and getting closer every second. Nicholas braced himself, ready to run.

But before he could get to his feet, there was a movement in the doorway. Nicholas glanced up and saw the man he had spotted just before the two cars had arrived. The man must have been inside the warehouse. Like them, he had spied on the entire transaction. Now, as Worm and his companion moved leisurely toward them, the man sprinted away, disappeared around the corner of the warehouse and away down the street, his footsteps echoing in the night.

Nicholas turned back to Worm, expecting him to follow. But Worm was standing quite still. It was impossible to see in the darkness, but he thought that Worm was smiling.

"Leave him!" The two words were careless, almost jocular. Worm and his companion turned around again and, more quickly now, made their way toward the boat.

"Well, that's a bit of . . ." Linda began in a breathless whisper.

The man's footsteps were already distant, but suddenly they stopped. Then they started again. Nicholas felt his skin crawl. The man was running *back*, back toward them. And now there was another sound. It was the last sound he had expected to hear in New York, and for that reason alone it caused a dark pool of dread to well up inside him. It was the sound of horses' hooves.

At first he tried to persuade himself that it was a policeman . . . perhaps two or three of them. But there were too many of them to be policemen. They were riding in formation, down from the Brooklyn Bridge. And there were more . . . coming the other way. Whoever the man was, the man who had unwittingly saved them, he was trapped between them. Nicholas could no longer hear his footsteps. The hooves striking concrete were like knives, slashing at the darkness. A gust of wind tugged at the collar of his shirt. It was icy cold.

And then he saw them.

They were shaped like men but they were not men. Dressed in moldering rags, they rode night-black horses, clutching at reins that hung in shreds, like seaweed. Each one held a spear, a twisted length of iron tapering to a jagged point. Their faces were hooded, hidden but for the dull orange glow of their eyes and the white smoke of the breath that curled around their lips. The eyes of the horses glowed, too, the same ugly orange. The horses were grotesquely thin, diseased. Their skin seemed to be stretched tight over their ribs, as if their innards had been torn out and the hide sewn back over a hollow shell.

They had formed themselves into a V, like the point of an arrow. There were five of them in this first group, two on each side of the leader, who rode at the front. He drew level with the barrels and stopped, the other four horses straddling the street. Nicholas could imagine five more riders waiting opposite them, outside his range of vision. The man from the warehouse had to be trapped somewhere between them.

The leader turned his head. Nicholas could almost hear the bones in his neck grinding. Then, for a terrible moment, the orange eyes locked into his and he could feel them boring into his skull. He wanted to scream, to run. He could feel Linda's hand clamping his own so tight that the blood could no longer circulate. His heart was a battering ram against his chest. He realized he had stopped breathing. His head was spinning and he sucked desperately for air. Still the eyes were fixed on his. With a huge effort he managed to look down, breaking the contact.

It was enough. The leader lifted his spear: a signal. At once the five horsemen charged forward, mercifully hidden from sight by the bulk of the warehouse.

There was a single, short scream.

It was an hour before Linda and Nicholas left their place of concealment. It was an hour before they could even move.

= THIRTEEN =

Grand Central Station

"THEY WEREN'T HUMAN. What were they? They weren't human. . . ."

Linda had been saying the same thing over and over again. She had sat through the entire night, drinking endless cups of tea while Nicholas had dozed fitfully on her bed. Only when the first streaks of dawn had filtered through the sky had she herself slept, a sleep disturbed by visions of black horses and rusting iron spears.

And now it was midday. She and Nicholas were sitting at the table in her apartment, avoiding each other's eyes. Linda produced a stale cigarette. She lit it and coughed, her eyes watering.

"What am I doing?" she muttered. She crushed the cigarette out. "I haven't smoked for ten years." She glanced at Nicholas. "What were they, Nick?"

"The Old Ones."

"*What* old ones?"

"I told you. In my dream . . ."

Linda stood up and carried an empty mug back into the kitchen. She set it down with a loud clatter. Nicholas looked at her thoughtfully.

"It's too much," she said. "I can just about cope with heroin smuggling, kidnapping, telepathy, murder—but when you start adding on dreams and devils . . . It's too much, Nicholas. It's crazy."

"Well, you saw them."

"It was a trick. It had to be some sort of trick."

Nicholas felt tired and depressed. It was almost as if Linda were blaming him for the events of the night before, indeed, for everything that had happened since they had met. Her apartment was small, but now it was positively claustrophobic. Despite everything they had done, they had gotten precisely nowhere. They still had no idea where Jeremy was. Worse still, there didn't seem to be anything left for them to do.

The telephone rang. Linda's answering machine was switched on, but she picked it up and pressed a button before the tape could turn. "Hello?" she said. Her face changed. "Yes?" There was a long silence as she listened. "But . . . yes, yes, of course. Right away." She put the receiver down.

"Who was it?" Nicholas asked.

"I don't believe it." Linda stared at the telephone as if she had never seen one before. "That was Ellen Levine."

"Who's she?"

"Only one of New York's top literary agents. Somehow she's gotten hold of a copy of my manuscript. She wants me to have lunch with her."

"That's great." Nicholas smiled. "When are you going?"

"She wants to see me right away." Linda shook her head. "But I can't . . . not after what's happened."

"Why not?"

"I just can't. I don't even want to leave the apartment."

Nicholas sighed. He picked up the manuscript of Linda's novel. Gently, he pressed it into her hands. "Look," he said. "Nothing can happen in broad daylight, and this is the chance you've been waiting for. You can't let my problems muck up your career. Go and have lunch with her. It'll do you good to get away from me for a while. I'm nothing but trouble."

Linda took the manuscript and smiled. "You're right," she said. "All except for the last bit. I could do with a break from all this. But Nick, don't leave here while I'm gone. Remember, you're the one these . . . Old Ones are after, not me."

"I'll stay here."

"Right." Linda paused, her hand brushing the tangles of her hair. "My God! I must look a wreck. And today of all days!"

Ten minutes later Linda hurried out wearing her best dress

and clutching the manuscript under her arm. Nicholas was glad to see her go. For some reason he wanted to be by himself. He found the file she had shown him in Central Park and opened it, flicking through the pages until he arrived at the clipping that concerned Martin Hopkins, the boy that Linda had said was now in Peru. He read the newspaper story. It told how an oil tanker had crashed into Martin's school in Yorkshire, England; how Martin had seen the accident before it happened and therefore been able to save the staff and eight hundred pupils. Nicholas examined the photograph above the article. If he had ever doubted the dream that had taken him to the edge of that mysterious sea, he did so no longer. The boy in the dream and the face in the photograph were the same.

The telephone rang again. Nicholas answered it.

"Hello? Is that Nicholas Helsey?" It was a female voice that he vaguely recognized, but he paused before answering. Who knew that he could be contacted in Linda's apartment?

"Who is it?" he asked.

"Nicholas . . . this is Evelyn."

"Evelyn?"

"We met at Radio City. Surely you remember . . . Mrs. Carnitt."

"Of course."

"Listen, Nicholas. I've good news. I've found your brother—Jeremy."

Nicholas felt his heart leap. "Jeremy? Where is he?"

"I can't tell you on the phone. It's too dangerous. But you and Linda have to come and meet me now. I'll be at the Oyster Bar in Grand Central Station. We can meet outside."

"Linda isn't here," Nicholas said, cursing the literary agent for choosing that moment to call. "She won't be back for a couple of hours."

"It'll be too late by then. You'll have to come alone." There was a moment's silence. Then Mrs. Carnitt spoke again. "If everything works out, I'll be there with your brother."

"But how . . . ? What . . . ?" There were a hundred questions Nicholas wanted to ask. How had Mrs. Carnitt managed to find him? What was the danger she had spoken of?

But Mrs. Carnitt had cut in too quickly. "The Oyster Bar at one o'clock," she said. "Can you find it?"

"Yes."

"Then be there."

The line went dead.

Nicholas looked at his watch. It was already twenty to one. There wasn't even time to leave a note for Linda. He would have to call her from the station. "I'll be there with your brother." The words still rang in his ears. Somehow, with all her contacts, Mrs. Carnitt had managed to find Jeremy. Hurriedly, Nicholas put on his parka and ran out of the apartment.

One million people pass through the vast central concourse of Grand Central Station every day of the week, bustling underneath the giant ceiling, with its 2,500 golden stars, and streaming into the passageways that lead to the trains. It is much more than just a station. It's home to seventy or more shops, to restaurants and stands, even to the world's largest clock.

The clock was showing a few minutes after one when Nicholas reached the Oyster Bar. It had been almost impossible to find in the labyrinth of underground tunnels, and in his haste he hadn't even thought of asking someone the way. But he was there. Resting against the glass doors that led into the restaurant, he tried to catch his breath. There was an archway spanning across the entrance above his head. To his left and right were two stairways, leading down—presumably to the platforms, for a constant flow of people passed by on both sides. Beyond the archway was a wide passageway with another, grander staircase leading up to the main concourse.

He glanced at his watch. He was only five minutes late, but suddenly he was afraid that he had missed them, that they had been and gone. He gazed through the glass doors and into the restaurant. There were about sixty tables there, each one covered with a bright checkered cloth. A white-coated waiter stood opposite the entrance, waiting to welcome anyone coming in to eat. The Oyster Bar was only half full. There was no sign of Jeremy or Mrs. Carnitt.

Even as he looked, it struck him as a strange place to meet. He hadn't thought of it on the telephone—Mrs. Carnitt hadn't given him the chance. But why here? If she had found

Jeremy, it seemed the last place to bring him. Whatever had happened to him, he would hardly be wanting lunch . . . and certainly not oysters. At the same time, Mrs. Carnitt knew that he was wanted by the police. Why had she asked him to come—and alone—to a place where he had every chance of being spotted?

Every instinct told him to get away. He was still poised, about to run, when the door of the Oyster Bar opened. A man stepped out, brushing against him.

"Here you are, kid," he heard the man say.

Something wet and metallic was pressed into his hand. He took it. He looked down. His hands were stained red. He twisted around to shout at the man who had spoken to him, but already he had gone. Nicholas looked down again. He was holding a knife.

At that moment, a black woman, old and fat, dressed in a heavy coat, appeared at the top of the staircase. He saw her just as she opened her mouth to scream.

"Help! Help!" The words echoed in the passageways. "Oh, please! No! Help!"

She dropped her arms. The front of her coat had been slashed with a knife. Blood was welling out.

And Nicholas was holding a knife.

There was blood on his hands.

Nicholas was like a caged animal. He was hemmed in by people on both sides, frozen in the act of climbing the stairs. Behind him the customers of the Oyster Bar had paused in the middle of their meals, their faces turning toward him while the waiter moved cautiously toward the door. There were people in the passageway, too, still silent, their faces filled with accusation. And the black woman was still screaming and sobbing. She had dropped to her knees, her hand clutching her stomach, her mouth gaping open and shut like a fish on dry land. Her screams were everywhere. Nicholas looked at the knife with horror. He spun around in a wild arc. The people recoiled. They were afraid of him.

"My money!" the black woman wailed. "He took it. Help!"

The crowd closed in on him. Nicholas swung the knife and for a moment they shrunk away. But it was the worst thing he could have done. If they needed any more convincing that he was a crazed juvenile thief and killer, he had just persuaded them.

"This way!" somebody shouted. "Over here!"

Nicholas looked up. Two uniformed policemen were making their way down the central staircase, alerted by the commotion. Both were armed. Making an instant decision, Nicholas sprinted forward, then away to the right. The crowd melted away from him.

He ran, the cries of the black woman lost in the general confusion behind him. The passageway sloped upwards past a row of metal lockers. People coming the other way stopped and stared at him. It took him a moment to realize that he was still carrying the knife. Angrily, he threw it away. It slid along the floor, leaving a bloody streak.

But the moment he lost the knife, the crowd lost its fear. Ahead of him, three burly men in overalls barred the way, their fists raised. His eyes darted to the left, searching for a way of escape. There was a staircase leading up. Dodging around the nearest of the three men, he took it two steps at a time.

The first thing he saw at the top was a bank of telephone booths. He was on the same level as the main concourse, separated from it by another archway, and there were people everywhere. But even among the milling crowd he could make out the blue uniforms of more policemen, drawn toward the Oyster Bar by radio contact. He made for the telephones, two thoughts uppermost in his mind. In the relative shelter of the booths he would be hidden, at least for a while. Nobody would think of looking for him there. And he had to get through to Linda. Now at last, when it was too late, everything was beginning to make sense.

He went into the first free booth and snatched up a receiver, grateful for the curving panel that concealed his head. His hand reached into his pocket and he scooped out a mass of loose change. With desperate fingers he found a coin, forced it into the slot, dialed. There was a click, then the single bleep of the dial tone. The telephone rang twice before it was answered.

"Hello. This is Linda Thorn. I'm afraid I'm not in right now, but if you leave a number, I'll call you back as soon as I can."

Nicholas was beginning to sweat. How long did the message on her answering machine go on?

"You have three minutes in which to leave your message. Please speak after the tone."

There was a long silence. Then another bleep.

"Linda . . ." Nicholas began, his voice soft and urgent. "I went out. It was a trap." He looked over his shoulder. There were still policemen in sight. "Don't trust Evelyn Carnitt," he said, and even as he spoke the words he realized the sick joke that was her name. "Evil incarnate," he repeated. "That's what she is. She's behind it all."

A policeman had appeared at the far end of the bank of telephones. He was slowly making his way toward Nicholas.

"A Bible . . ." he continued breathlessly. "Joe Fanelli tried to take a clue. Look at the page from the Bible. And I know where Jeremy is. I know! There's an island in the East River, reached by a cable car. That's what I saw, Linda. I saw the cable car. The boat from the market . . . it went to the island. Find the island, Linda, and you've found Jeremy. But don't trust Evelyn Carnitt. . . ."

There was nothing more he could say. The policeman was too close. Dropping the telephone, he turned and ran.

He passed underneath the archway and continued into the main concourse. Suddenly he felt very small, dwarfed by the huge surroundings. There were people moving in every conceivable direction, heading toward corridors and separate concourses, tubes and tunnels, staircases and the escalators that soared upward into the Pan Am Building above. The great brick cavern was filled with echoes: echoes of voices, babbling and indistinct, echoes of a thousand feet pattering across the white stone floor. He pressed forward, past the circular information booth and on toward the far end. He had to keep moving. It didn't matter where he went.

He had gotten as far as a café on a raised terrace at the end of the concourse before he was spotted. Above the café was a window, the biggest window Nicholas had ever seen, shaped like something out of a monstrous cathedral. The window was barred and the bars reminded him of the prison cell that must surely await him. The blood had dried on his hands. He had left smears of it on the telephone. He wondered if the black woman had died.

"There he is!"

The voice boomed out of the crowd and suddenly he was exposed, caught in the open, halfway up the station's widest staircase. It was the signal the police had been waiting for. Looking back, he could see dozens of them, running from every side, guns raised. Somebody fired a shot. A bullet slammed into the concrete inches from him, sending chips flying. People began to scream. In the café a waiter pushing a cart piled high with plates of food dived for cover, sending the cart hurtling out of control into a cigarette machine, sandwiches and cakes splattering onto the floor.

Nicholas spotted an open door on the edge of the café and made for it. A second waiter tried to block the way. He pushed. The man lost his balance and crashed into a table which collapsed beneath him. He knew now that it was hopeless, that he couldn't get away. But still he ran, refusing to give in.

The door led him into a service area. A man in a guard's uniform appeared, walking toward him.

"What do you think . . . ?" he began.

Nicholas ran past him and up yet another staircase. A few seconds later the police had reached the door.

"Up there!" the guard yelled. "He went that way!"

Three floors up Nicholas paused for breath. Behind the scenes at Grand Central Station everything was dark and grimy. There was no way out, and the higher he went, the less chance he would have of finding one. The police were only two floors below him. He could hear their footsteps on the stairs. There were a dozen or more of them, and now they had slowed down. They knew he was trapped.

He tried a last doorway. This one led him into a narrow passage enclosed by two walls of dirty glass. The floor was made of glass too. Nicholas moved forward slowly, fascinated despite himself. Everywhere he looked there were iron girders and levers, joined together by a network of cogs and chains. It was as if he had stumbled into the inside of some Victorian machine.

A policeman appeared at the bottom of the passage. He crouched on one knee, his gun held at arm's length, pointing at Nicholas. Nicholas looked behind him. Two more policemen were standing there, also aiming at him. Nobody spoke.

Nicholas gazed through the glass. And he realized where he was.

He was inside the window. For the windows of Grand Central Station were made of two sheets of glass, separated by a narrow corridor. Nicholas was standing in that corridor. He could see the crowd staring up at him. There was the departures board, the Kodak slide, a glowing advertisement for the magazine, *Newsweek*. The clock above the information booth read 1:25. The amplified voice rumbled in the air. Another train was about to leave.

It was another world on the other side of the window. The real world. But it was no longer his world.

Nicholas stretched out his hands against the glass and sank to his knees. He had nowhere to run.

= FOURTEEN =

The Old Ones

LINDA WALKED INTO the office in Radio City and sat down on one of the silk-covered chairs. Evelyn Carnitt was waiting for her behind the desk, her perfectly manicured fingers resting on the smooth, polished surface.

"I'm sorry it's taken me so long to see you, my dear," she said. Her arms remained on the desk, but she lifted her fingers in a gesture of apology. "I've been busy. Our show here is about to finish. The time has come to move on to the next stage in our . . . operations."

"Nicholas . . ." Linda began.

"Ah, yes! Young Nicholas Helsey." Mrs. Carnitt looked sadly at Linda, as if a doctor were about to tell someone he had a fatal disease. "It really is a great shame," she said.

Two days had passed since Linda had gotten back from an appointment with a literary agent who had never heard of her and who certainly didn't have a copy of her manuscript. With the first stirrings of panic, she had hurried back to her apartment to find the door forced open, the place empty. At first she had thought that Nicholas had been kidnapped like his brother, but there was no evidence of a fight. Everything seemed just as she had left it. So who had broken in, and why?

She had gone through the apartment while she waited for Nicholas, pulling open drawers and cupboards, trying to discover what had been taken. She was playing the radio while she searched and it was on the radio that she heard the news:

a chase in Grand Central Station, the so-called telepathic twin arrested. Hardly believing what she was hearing, Linda had moved to the telephone to make a call. That was when she had found what the intruder had taken.

The tape was missing from the answering machine.

She had called Evelyn Carnitt.

"Nicholas was framed," Linda insisted now. "They used a trick to get me out of the apartment and then somehow got him to leave. He must have left a message for me on my answering machine."

"What was it?" Mrs. Carnitt asked.

Linda signed. "I don't know. It was stolen before I got back."

Evelyn Carnitt leaned back in her chair. Her fingers had woven themselves together on the desk. "I'm sorry, my dear," she said. "Your friend did attack that woman. He's already pleaded guilty."

"But that's impossible!" Linda cried.

"What's more, it now turns out that he was also responsible for the death of his uncle, Don White." Mrs. Carnitt's deep black eyes challenged Linda to argue. "He's admitted that too. It seems that little Nicholas Helsey has been leading you up the garden path."

"I don't believe it," Linda said angrily.

"Nicholas has a disturbed mind, Linda," Mrs. Carnitt explained, her voice full of sympathy. "He's sick. That's why his brother, Jeremy, ran away. He was afraid of him. You should consider yourself lucky that he never turned on you."

Linda got to her feet. She had heard enough.

"You've got it all wrong," she said. "I'm going to the police. I'll soon tell them—"

"That would be very unwise, my dear." Suddenly the voice was hard. Too hard. Linda glanced at Mrs. Carnitt curiously, remembering how Nicholas had mistrusted her. But then the older woman smiled again, standing up herself and moving around the desk. "You can't get involved," she continued. "Don't forget . . . when you were hiding Nicholas, you were breaking the law. If you go to the police now, you'll only get yourself into trouble."

"But I can't just leave him in jail," Linda protested.

"Nicholas isn't in jail . . . exactly."

Evelyn Carnitt paused at the corner of the desk. The golden clusters below her ears swayed as she shook her head.

"As soon as I heard he had been arrested, I got to work," she explained. "I told you . . . I have a certain influence with the New York police. I genuinely liked the child and I wanted to help. So I managed to short-circuit the usual procedure and have him sent to a rather special place. Do you know Roosevelt Island?"

"I've heard of it," Linda said.

"There's a prison there—just opposite the United Nations. About three hundred young offenders are housed there. The law would call them juvenile criminals, but I prefer to look on them simply as misguided children. That's why my charity—the Golden Cup—recently came to an arrangement with the state. In essence, we took over the administration of the prison. We now run it. And we try to make it more of a hospital than a detention center. Of course, the children are locked up. They have to be. But they're well cared for.

"I managed to get Nicholas transferred to Roosevelt Island. So you don't have to worry about him, my dear. He's in my care. . . ."

The room measured ten paces by six paces. Nicholas knew. He had walked back and forth a hundred times. Sitting on the narrow bunk beneath the barred window, he wondered if Jeremy had once occupied it. He was certain that Jeremy was near, somewhere on the island. But he couldn't feel him . . . and that worried him even more than his own predicament.

He understood so much now. When he had first made contact with his brother that night in Linda's apartment, he had sensed that he was flying—but not in a plane or a helicopter. That only left a cable car—and he had seen it crossing the East River on his way back in the taxi from Radio City. But at that time, exhausted after his fight with Worm, he had been unable to make the connection. And the torn page from the Bible, carried by Joe Fanelli. That had been another clue, and it had been under his nose from the very start. The page had told of "a golden cup, full of abominations." The Golden Cup was the name of Carnitt's charity. The abominations were heroin.

He had been taken around part of the island by a mirthlessly smiling Mr. Banes. Only then had the full extent of Mrs. Carnitt's operation become clear. The prisoners in Block A, some as young as eleven and twelve, were little more than slaves, working in the printing room, where thousands of Bibles were being produced.

But even they didn't know what then happened. Every night the Bibles were removed, carried to a basement by the guards. There the pages were cut out to produce a secret hollow. And in another, galleried room, dozens more guards were also at work, crouched over piles of white powder; weighing it, dividing it, diluting it, and finally shoveling it into plastic bags.

It was a smuggling operation on a massive scale—children being the perfect camouflage of a juvenile prison.

It was in Block A that Nicholas's own cell was located. For some reason Mr. Banes had been ordered to keep him away from the building where Linda's missing children—the ones with powers—were housed. But he had glimpsed it from the outside and he had been told about the Treatment Center. Even the name made his blood run cold. Had his brother been there? What had they done to him? All his questions about Jeremy were ignored.

Left alone, he had more time to worry about himself. Mr. Banes had told him that the island would soon be shut down, its usefulness ended. He was well aware that Mrs. Carnitt wouldn't leave any witnesses alive. The fact that he had been kept away from the other "specials" disturbed him. Clearly, they had no use for him. He was nothing more than a nuisance, brought there simply to be gotten rid of.

But at least he had gotten through to Linda before he was taken. That was something to be grateful for. Even now she would be rallying to his aid. The missing paranormal children, the torn page from the Bible, the heroin smuggling, the Golden Cup . . . the whole thing made sense only when you added Evelyn Carnitt. Somehow Linda would find a way to reach him. He just hoped she would come in time.

Linda Thorn was worried. As she left Radio City, her mind was a whirl of contradictory thoughts. Mrs. Carnitt had said that she could see Nicholas—perhaps in a week, perhaps a little longer. She had promised to call as soon as a visit could be arranged. But somehow the promise didn't ring true. Nothing about the woman quite rang true.

"That would be very unwise, my dear."

The words had been hastily spoken, and Mrs. Carnitt had recovered with equal speed, but at that moment her mask had slipped. And that face, with its perfect makeup, not a hair out of place, was a mask. Linda was certain of it now. What lay behind it? She wasn't sure, but it was as if she had glimpsed the skeleton beneath the flesh and she was still reeling from the shock.

Mrs. Carnitt . . .

Much of her work concerned children, and children were missing. The rehabilitation center that she had mentioned—that, too, struck a chord. It was on Roosevelt Island. And Roosevelt Island was just upriver from the Fulton Fish Market. And Joe Fanelli. The East River had become his grave. Could he have been a prisoner on the island? He had been carrying a page from a Bible—and that was another link with Mrs. Carnitt. Linda remembered some of the words on the page . . . something about a golden cup. . . .

Mrs. Carnitt . . . Mrs. Carnitt! Linda knew her enemy now, but the knowledge brought only a wave of hopelessness. How could she, an unpublished novelist, take on one of the most powerful and celebrated women in the United States, a woman who had dined at the White House and who had been honored by just about every government leader abroad? Who would possibly believe her?

Linda was so absorbed in her thoughts that she didn't hear the car idling close to the curb as it followed her along Fifth Avenue. She only noticed it when, with a screech of its tires, it sped ahead, then cut in at an angle toward the sidewalk. A door opened and a man in a dark suit and dark glasses got out.

"Miss Thorn?" he asked.

"Yes . . ."

"Will you get in, please."

There was no time to argue. Linda was bundled into the car. The man climbed in next to her, slamming the door. A moment later the car sped away.

* * *

They came for Nicholas later that same morning. Two guards led him out of Block A and across the parking lot to the gray brick building on Gallows Way, where Mr. Banes had his office. A huddled group of prisoners—boys of his own age—watched him curiously as he went, but none of them dared try to speak to him.

Evelyn Carnitt was waiting for him inside the office.

She was wearing a tight-fitting dress of black and scarlet, the colors complimenting her eyes and lips. Mr. Banes stood beside her, holding up a match while she puffed at a cigarette held in a long ivory holder. When Nicholas had first met her, she had made every effort to project a kindly, charitable persona. Now she hadn't just given way to evil. She was reveling in it.

Mr. Banes nodded at the guards, who forced Nicholas into a wooden chair in the middle of the room, tying his hands to the arms. He didn't even try to struggle. He had no chance. It was better to conserve his strength for later. The guards finished their work and left the room. At last Evelyn Carnitt spoke.

"The second of the five," she said.

"Where's Jeremy?" Nicholas demanded. "What have you done with him?"

Mrs. Carnitt arched an eyebrow and blew out a thin stream of smoke. "You have courage, boy," she said. "And I almost admire your pathetic loyalty. You are minutes from death, yet you still think only of your brother."

"Where is he?"

Her eyes flashed, suddenly angry. Nicholas was helpless, her prisoner. Yet still he defied her. Even Mr. Banes looked thoughtfully at him.

"Do you know who I am?" she hissed.

"You are one of the Old Ones." Nicholas trembled inside as he spoke the words, but he was determined not to show her that he was afraid.

"One of the Old Ones?" Mrs. Carnitt threw back her head and laughed. "I am the Queen of the Old Ones," she cried. "The Old Ones serve me as does your brother, Jeremy." She leaned forward, the tip of the cigarette only inches from Nicholas's face. "Your brother is no longer here and he is no longer your brother. Jeremy is mine."

She waved the cigarette and Mr. Banes snatched up an ashtray, holding it out for her. She tapped the end and glowing ash fell, not into the glass bowl but onto his wrist, burning the skin. But Mr. Banes did not move. Mrs. Carnitt laughed again.

"I would enjoy turning you," she began. "It would give me pleasure to make you into my creature. But you have already caused me enough inconvenience and you arrive just as my work is about to reach fruition. Three days from now the United States is going to be swamped by a wave of destruction that will make the plague look like a dose of flu in a kindergarten. Three days from now . . . Do you know what that is?"

"Thursday?" Nicholas muttered.

The corner of Mr. Banes's mouth flickered into the beginnings of a smile. Mrs. Carnitt glanced sharply at him. He forced himself to remain impassive. Her cigarette was almost half finished. Soon she would stub it out. And if he angered her, she wouldn't use the ashtray.

"It is November twenty-second," Mrs. Carnitt snapped. "Thanksgiving Day. The day that celebrates the birth of America. But this year it will be the day that marks America's end."

She gestured, and Mr. Banes pulled up a second chair so that she could sit down close to Nicholas. He shuddered as he looked at her face. At close quarters it was curiously hideous. It was as if the eyes, the nose, and the mouth had been surgically positioned. It was all too precise, too perfect. Even the skin was without blemish: a smooth, dead white.

"The Old Ones ruled the world in the beginning of time," she continued. "We were the first great evil, and our influence has been felt across the globe throughout the history of mankind. Have you ever wondered, Nicholas, why there have been so many battles, so many wars? Have you ever wondered why one half of the planet pays to destroy its great piles of surplus food while the other half starves? Why have animals and plants been wiped out, killed by pollution? Why have scientists built weapons that can destroy the world when they haven't even found a cure for the common cold?

"That is the voice of the Old Ones, Nicholas. It is still being heard after all the millions of years.

"But we have been forced to work from a distance. Before your so-called civilization began, five rose up against us . . . five children. A terrible war was fought, a war we should have won. But we were defeated by a trick, and banished from the world, forced into a separate dimension, the way barred by two mystic gates. One of these gates was in Yorkshire, the other in Peru. And for centuries afterward our disciples—warlocks and wizards, witches and black magicians . . . they had many names—sought to open the gates to let us back into a world that was rightfully ours.

"One of them almost succeeded in Yorkshire. For a few seconds the gate was open. But the five had risen again. A boy called Martin Hopkins was brought to the gate by the very people who had most reason to fear him. He was only thirteen years old and he was alone. But still he had the power to defeat us. The gate was closed and we were driven back.

"He was less successful the second time. Somehow he found his way to Peru, where the second gate was about to open, unlocked by an alignment of the stars. He was aided by another of the five, and between them they were able to challenge us. Another of our disciples was killed. Our king was wounded. But this time they weren't strong enough to close the gate. It remained open. And the Old Ones returned.

"We are in the world now, at work in Europe, America . . . all the major continents. It will take us time to reestablish ourselves and we cannot be sure of success until the five no longer live to threaten us. But that is the key to it. There have to be five. Only when the five have come together will they have the power to defeat us, and I have made sure that that will never happen.

"In the past year I have been searching for children with . . . special abilities. I have found them across America and brought them here for examination. If I could get my hands on just one of the five, it would be enough to smash them forever. Martin Hopkins and his friend were already too strong to be taken without a fight. I was looking for the three children who did not know what they were, who they were. And I found Jeremy . . . and you.

"Jeremy is mine now. He will serve me until I tire of him

and have him killed. You will be dead by then yourself. Your death is here, in this room.

"And then it will begin. The world may lean toward evil, but there are still those who fight it. It is the youth of the world that we must deal with first, the children, with their ideals and optimism. We are about to crush them, Nicholas. And in three days time we can start.

"In the past six months I have amassed a huge store of heroin . . . more than has ever been seen in one place at one time. It is here, on this island. We have tons of it, paid for by the money raised by the Golden Cup. I have been helped by rich and powerful men; by politicians and industrialists . . . people whose greed has lent itself to my cause. Mr. Banes has shown you our workshops. The Golden Cup has promised that every child in America shall have a Bible. And inside every Bible will be concealed enough heroin to start a crime wave that will engulf the world.

"It was Marx who once said that religion is the opium of the people. I have taken him almost literally. Have you seen what hard drugs do to young people? They turn them into animals. Already there are tens of thousands of children who pay for the supposed pleasures of heroin. What do you think will happen when suddenly, in every town and on every street, it becomes freely available—and at a tenth of the normal price? It will be the beginning of anarchy. The whole fabric of society will tear itself apart. The children of the world will be ours.

"The heroin will leave here on Thanksgiving Day, carried by a fleet of trucks across state lines. The Golden Cup has been a perfect cover. Who would suppose that my trucks are the carriers of death? Who would dare search inside them? By the time anyone realizes what has happened, it will be too late.

"And your time has come too. Only one boy ever tried to escape from the island; a boy called Joe Fanelli. Heroin is a slow poison, but a large dose acts more quickly. Nobody asked any questions when he was found. He was just another dead addict. Nobody will ask any questions about you either. We'll do it now, Banes."

Evelyn Carnitt stubbed her cigarette out on the edge of Nicholas's chair and stood up while Mr. Banes moved forward. Nicholas recoiled, tugging at the arms of the chair, straining every muscle. But he was tied down too securely. Mr. Banes reached out for him, his hand clutching the sleeve of his shirt. Hooking his fingers, he pulled, ripping the sleeve away and exposing Nicholas's bare arm. Then he grabbed hold of it, his hand like a vice just below Nicholas's elbow, stopping the circulation of his blood.

At the same time, Evelyn Carnitt had opened a drawer in the desk and taken out a hypodermic syringe. Coldly, efficiently, she held it up to the light, pressing the plunger to send a tiny fountain of transparent liquid squirting out of the needle. Nicholas looked down at his arm, still clamped by Mr. Banes. The veins were standing out under his skin. He watched as Evelyn Carnitt approached. He couldn't believe what was being done to him. He didn't want to believe it.

The point of the needle touched his skin. He rocked back and forth, slamming his shoulders into the chair. He was shouting now, the words incoherent. But Mr. Banes held him fast, the arm locked in his hand.

"Good-bye, Nicholas," Mrs. Carnitt said.

He felt the prick as the needle slid into his flesh. He felt the liquid enter his bloodstream and course upward into his brain. He heard Evelyn Carnitt's soft laughter in his ear as the needle came out.

Then there was nothing.

= FIFTEEN =

The First Circle

"I'M DEAD," NICHOLAS muttered to himself.

He was lying on a rocky platform at the foot of a mountain. He sat up, the dust and pebbles rolling off his back. He didn't feel dead. His body was aching and there was a dull pain in his arm, but otherwise he felt fresh and alert. He looked down at himself. He was wearing the same clothes that he had worn on the island. The sleeve of his shirt had been torn off. He raised his arm. There was a small puncture between his wrist and the crease in the arm, and a small dribble of dried blood. He remembered what had been done to him—but what *had* been done to him?

They had injected him with enough heroin to kill him almost instantly. There had been no last-minute rescue or reprieve. It followed then that he must be dead. But if he was dead, was he in heaven or hell? His eyes swept across the landscape. Wherever he was, it didn't look like either . . . but for that matter it didn't look anything like the world.

The mountain sloped down to the shore of a lake, its water a purer blue than he had ever seen. All the colors were strange and unworldly. A ribbon of vivid pink stretched itself over the horizon, melting into a sort of turquoise and then a darker blue above. The clouds were more silver than white. In the distance, far beyond the other side of the lake, a volcano jutted into the sky, black smoke belching out of its jagged crown and a stream of burning crimson lava winding its way down into the valley below.

Plants grew on the shores of the lake, but they were like no plants that Nicholas had ever seen. Again, the color was wrong. The green was too intense. And the leaves formed fantastic, impossible shapes. Some of the plants were sprawled across the sand as if they had just staggered out of the lake itself, while others were still half-submerged in the water, the leaves groping like fingers over the land.

There was a splash, and Nicholas's eyes were drawn to a creature just beside the shore. As he watched, it extended four flipperlike legs and began to crawl out of the water toward him. It was gray, with the body, scales, and fins of a fish, but with the wrinkled head of a lizard and the eyes of a snake. Two more creatures followed it, breaking through the surface of the water. Nicholas blinked. Where was he? What was going on?

He heard a flutter in the air and looked up. The sun . . . but this wasn't the sun. It was a vast ball of fire. He could actually see the flames rippling out. A flock of birds flew past. There was something snakelike about them, too, for their bodies extended far from their heads, with long, arched necks and clawlike feet hanging below. Their plumage was orange and blue, their eyes a glittering green. Nicholas didn't have to be an expert to know that the birds didn't exist in the world that he was familiar with.

He was struck by an unpleasant thought. He had once read that drugs like heroin cause hallucinations. That was one of the reasons why people took them in the first place. Perhaps everything he was seeing was a hallucination.

In which case, if he wasn't actually dead, he could still be dying.

Something moved behind him and he turned around to find himself facing an old man dressed in rags, supporting himself on a thick staff. The man was virtually blind. He stared at Nicholas with eyes that were covered with lifeless white cataracts, his face drawn haggard by suffering and self-pity. The rags hung loose from his emaciated body, but they were wound tightly around one leg, where they ended just below the knee.

"Boy!" he wheezed in a thin, quivering voice. He stretched out one grimy hand as if begging for alms. "Have pity . . . pity on an old man, a victim of the Old Ones."

"The Old Ones . . ."

"They took my eyes. Tell me, boy . . . you seem kind. You wouldn't hurt an old man. Are you a servant of the Old Ones?"

"No. . . ." Nicholas shook his head. "No!"

"Then you must die."

What happened next was so sudden, so unexpected, that Nicholas could only stand and stare, convinced that he was dreaming. The image of the old beggar rippled like a reflection in water. The rags disappeared. The white eyes burned red. The neck seemed to sprout upward, the head bulging and cracking open. A moment later the beggar was gone and in his place stood a soldier, seven feet tall, encased in dull silver armor. From the shoulders down he was a giant of a man. Above the shoulders the head of a monster lunged forward on a twisting neck. Crocodile teeth jutted in glistening points from an elongated mouth. A forked tongue flickered, gluelike saliva trickling out of one corner. The creature breathed from nostrils set in an uneven bulge high up in his forehead. The staff was still there, but now it was metallic and studded with rusting nails.

"You must die," it repeated, but now the words bubbled out on a cloud of rancid breath.

The creature leaped forward, using both legs to propel itself, like a giant toad. Its tongue spat out, the saliva frothing. At the same time, it swung the staff, the nails ripping through the air. Nicholas jerked back. It was a dream. It had to be a dream. But he knew that if he allowed the creature to reach him, he would never wake up.

It landed, swung around, lunged again with the staff. This time one of the nails made contact, tearing his shirt and gashing his skin. Nicholas pressed a hand against the wound, looking down as blood welled through his fingers. The blood was real enough. The creature laughed, a soft gurgling. Its head lashed from side to side, the eyes aglow. The fiery sun glinted off its armor. It was holding the staff in both hands now, using it like a battering ram, shuffling forward an inch at a time. Nicholas moved back, felt his foot come down on a loose rock, lost his balance. He crashed to the ground and a moment later the creature was standing over him, silhouetted against the sun, the staff stretching up to the very sky.

"Die . . . die . . . die . . . die . . ." it chanted.

And then the creature shrieked. Nicholas hadn't seen or heard anything, but suddenly there was a thin shaft of wood sticking out of its neck. It dropped the staff, its hands grappling upward, writhing in agony. Black blood fountained out of it, splashing onto Nicholas. For a moment it swayed on its two legs, the mouth opening and shutting, snapping at the air. Then it fell to one side, sprawling in the dust.

Nicholas sat up. A boy stood a little farther up the mountain, lowering a bow, a second arrow already in his hand in case the first had missed. Nicholas glanced at the creature. The boy had no need to worry. The arrow had flown at an angle, hitting its target just above the level of the jaw and slanting down into its throat. As the boy scrambled down the slope, Nicholas got to his feet, wiping the black ooze off his face.

The boy was about his own age, dark-haired, Hispanic. He was wearing brown leather trousers and a tunic belted at the waist. Now he was looking at Nicholas with a mixture of pleasure and disbelief. He still gripped the bow as if prepared to use it. But seeing that Nicholas was unarmed, he slid the arrow back into the quiver that was strapped to his back.

"Nicholas . . . ?" he asked.

"You know me."

"I know you . . . I don't know you. I don't get it. . . ."

"Who are you?"

"Pedro." The boy kicked at the creature's body, making sure that it was indeed dead.

"What is it?" Nicholas asked. "What was it?" he corrected himself.

"A Shape-Changer," Pedro replied. He glanced up and smiled. "Martin sent me. He said you'd be here."

"Martin?" It took Nicholas a few seconds to understand. "Then you're one of the five."

"The five?" Pedro sighed, and suddenly there was pain in his eyes. "There were five, but . . ."

"Where am I?" Nicholas demanded. "What's going on?"

"It's not easy. Look"—Pedro gestured back up the mountain—"we can talk as we go. We can't stay here. There's no time."

Together the two boys made their way up a zigzagging path

that had been cut into the side of the mountain. Neither of them spoke. The path climbed steeply to begin with. At times they had to use both hands and feet to pull themselves up. The mountain was bare and barren, the rock a powdery gray, but here and there thistles sprouted out of the ground, dark green, flecked with tiny white flowers.

"Don't touch them," Pedro warned as his hand came to rest only inches from a clump. "They sting."

At last the path leveled out to a more gentle slope. About a mile ahead of them, between two mountain peaks, was a pass shaped like a saucer. Nicholas guessed they were heading for it. But he had no idea what he'd find on the other side. They stopped to catch their breath and Pedro unhooked a gourd from his belt, passing it to Nicholas.

"What is it?" Nicholas asked.

"Water," Pedro said. "But it's good."

It was. Despite the sun, it was icy cold. He drank his fill, then passed it back to Pedro, who drank in turn. Then he screwed the top back on and refastened it to the belt.

"Now we can talk," he said. He looked closely at Nicholas, still not sure of him. "I don't get it," he said. "But . . . listen . . ."

They set off again, Pedro talking as they went.

"We've been fighting the Old Ones for a year," he said. "Five of us traveled across the world. We had to come together. It was the only way we could win. And meanwhile the war went on. The Old Ones were strong. They ruled. Nothing could stop them.

"But even so, they couldn't rest. Not while we were alive . . . the five. Martin was our leader. There was me. Then the twins . . . Jeremy and Nicholas."

"Jeremy is here?" Nicholas interrupted.

"He's here," Pedro said. He frowned. "But let me explain. There were the twins, and Will, the last of the five. And at last we arrived in the same land. The end was near. The great darkness was drawn in. But at last we had arrived. We could join together, become one."

Pedro pointed. "It was arranged that we would meet in a place beyond the pass. That was where we would fight the last battle. That was where the circle would be formed.

"But at the last minute the Old Ones struck. They were

desperate now. Their forces were all over the place. The Shape-Changers too. They were asking questions, searching. They had to find us, you see. To kill one of us would be enough to break the circle. That was all they had to do. And they did.

"One of us was taken. He fought bravely—he and a few soldiers. But he was surrounded, outnumbered. All the power of the Old Ones was set against him. For six hours they fought, while the four of us who were left raced toward him. But by the time we reached him, it was too late. The boy was dead. His body was mutilated. They had done horrible things to him in death, Nicholas. I hope only that his end was swift. He was my friend.

"We took him back with us on a stretcher and buried him. We have mourned for him ever since. For him and for the world. That was yesterday, at sunset."

"Which one of the five was it?" Nicholas asked. "Who was killed?"

Pedro stopped and turned round.

"It was you."

Nicholas stood rigid, the wind blowing in his hair. Pedro reached out to touch him, but he backed away. Suddenly he was shivering. He didn't understand. He didn't understand any of it.

"Me?" he whispered.

"You don't remember?"

"No. You're wrong. This isn't my world. I don't belong here. Yesterday I was in New York."

Pedro shook his head. "I don't know that place." Nicholas said nothing, so he went on. "This morning Martin came to me. He told me where to go, where I would find you. I was to bring you to him. Like I say, Nicholas, I don't get it. But it is you. You're here, alive. It's—"

Pedro broke off. Nicholas could see that he was close to exhaustion. But there was something more. He was lost. Something magical had happened, something he couldn't understand.

At last he pulled himself together. "Come," he said. "We must go to Martin and we must go quickly."

They reached the pass and stopped again. Nicholas looked down. It was a sight he would never forget.

There was a great plateau on the other side of the pass, surrounded on three sides by mountains and stretching as far as the eye could see. Beneath the mountains there were trees, tropical palms and ferns, but the central area—a vast arena—was flat and bare. The sun had positioned itself above the exact center of the arena, the light of its flames beating down on the sand that rippled in the soft breeze.

To one side—on the right—there was an oasis, a circular pool of crystal water with a scattering of green vegetation. Here a group of white tents had been pitched, with white flags flapping above the entrances. Each flag bore the same simple device. A blue pentagram in a circle.

It was impossible to tell from that distance how many people there were, but the whole camp was a hive of activity. Small horses—or animals like them—were being saddled. People were running back and forth, snatching up weapons, forming themselves into lines. Nicholas caught a glint of silver as the sun reflected off a sword or shield. More people, women perhaps, were kneeling beside the oasis, filling gourds for the soldiers. A single figure was walking among the troops, stopping now and then to address a few words to the men. The figure was small: a boy.

Nicholas turned to Pedro. "Martin?" he asked.

Pedro nodded. "Yes." He touched Nicholas's arm. "Look there."

Nicholas followed his eye to the other side of the plateau. There was a strange darkness at the foot of the mountains. He had noticed it already, but had dismissed it as a shadow. Now he looked at it more closely. He drew in his breath.

The army of the Old Ones was huge. If there were perhaps five hundred people with Martin, here there were five thousand. And yet it was difficult to think of them as individuals. They were an army, a mass, an overwhelming blackness.

But even as he watched the army began to break apart as the troops moved into formation. First came the foot-soldiers, carrying axes and spears. With them were more of the Shape-Changers, clutching their metal staves, their lizard heads craning forward. To one side was a shape that he recognized: the riders, wrapped in their graveyard rags, their orange eyes burning beneath their hoods. The three squadrons formed a line that stretched for more than a mile, weaving away toward the horizon. Alone they would have the strength to destroy the opposing army in minutes. But they were only the advance guard.

Behind them came the animals, a sight beyond imagining. A spider the size of a house crawled forward, the black hair bristling on its eight legs, its poison sacs bulging underneath. A monkey, forty feet tall, bounded away, its tail pounding at the sand, its movements fast and jerky, like a mechanical toy. It raised a four-fingered hand and cocked its head, opened its mouth, and laughed. The sound was horrible, chilling . . . between a cackle and a scream. Something soared over one of the mountains. It was a bird, again of monstrous size. Its tattered wings hardly seemed to move, beating so slowly that Nicholas wondered how it could possibly fly.

But then everything was forgotten as he realized that it wasn't a mountain that the bird had just flown over. The mountain had moved. Before it had been crouching. Now it stood up.

The King of the Old Ones.

Nicholas covered his eyes, not daring to look. Blackness so deep as to be impenetrable. Two eyes glowing like hot coals. Arms shaped like those of a human with long webbed fingers and nails like scimitars. A mouth stretched in a voracious smile beneath a hooked beak. Spikes everywhere. A crown surmounted by two horns. These were the fragments that he would remember. The whole picture was too much for his mind to bear.

The two armies stood facing each other across the empty plateau. For a long minute everything was still.

"It's about to begin," Pedro said. "Be ready."

"To do what?"

"To run . . ."

When the attack began, it was so unexpected that for a moment Nicholas didn't believe what he was seeing. He had been waiting for the black army to sweep across the plateau, to bear down on Martin's forces from three sides. He had braced himself for what could only be a massacre. But it was happening the other way. The flea was attacking the tiger.

Three horsemen had ridden forward, each one carrying a standard with the blue pentagram. Nicholas felt an inner thrill. He was still too far away to see clearly, but the rider in the center had to be Martin. And Jeremy must be with him. Two more lines of mounted soldiers, perhaps a hundred strong, rode behind. And last of all, spreading across the field, were the infantry and archers, marching in time, their weapons raised.

From the other side of the plateau came a low rumble that built up to a deafening roar. The army of the Old Ones was laughing, their victory assured. Martin and his followers were committing suicide.

They were halfway across now, their horses cantering, picking up speed with every second that passed. The Old Ones waited to receive them. Still the gleeful shouting filled the air.

But then the three horses wheeled round and suddenly they were galloping away from the field, away toward the pass where Nicholas and Pedro stood.

The King of the Old Ones turned his head. The burning eyes sparked red.

He screamed, a sound that broke through the clamor of his soldiers and echoed all around.

And then Nicholas remembered what Evelyn Carnitt had told him. . . .

"A great war was fought, a war we should have won. But we were defeated, by a trick."

And at the same moment, he realized that he was witnessing that trick, that he was involved in it.

"Now!" Pedro shouted.

As one, Nicholas and Pedro sprinted down the slope toward the approaching riders. Together they ran, their feet kicking up the rubble. At the same time, the army of the Old Ones charged, thundering down on them from the left. But even as he raced forward, Nicholas was able to see just how brilliant Martin's strategy had been. His forces had also swung around, forming a barrier between the Old Ones and them. His archers were kneeling and a moment later the sky was darkened by a hail of arrows. The front line of foot-soldiers and Shape-Changers broke apart, bodies falling as the arrows found their targets, forming another obstacle for the troops directly behind.

Even so, it was going to be a close thing. Martin and his two outriders were still a hundred yards away. The black army was only a hundred yards behind them . . . just a few paces for the giant animals.

The bird was the first to reach them. Hearing its master's call, it had soared into the air and now it swooped down, diving out of the sun. Nicholas saw his brother just as Jeremy turned his back. He was holding a bow and arrow even as he rode, and now he aimed upward, fired. His arrow buried itself in one of the bird's swollen eyes. It lurched back as if it had been kicked, then plummeted down, crashing into the spider, its huge weight crushing two of the spider's legs.

That still left the monkey. It leaped, arcing over the two armies and landing in front of the three riders, between them and Nicholas and Pedro. Pedro's reactions were the faster of the two. Without breaking his pace he swerved around the monkey's leg. Nicholas skidded to a halt. A monstrous shadow hurtled toward him as the monkey's hand tried to swat him like an insect. Nicholas threw himself aside. The hand crashed into the sand and for a few precious seconds he was invisible, lost in a miniature sandstorm. He seized his chance, running forward between the monkey's legs. A moment later he was behind it, choking, the sand in his eyes, trying to get his bearings.

All he could see was the army of the Old Ones. They had completely overwhelmed Martin's fighters, crushing them underfoot in their desperation to reach the five. They were everywhere; the shrieking Riders, the Shape-Changers, the moldering foot-soldiers. Nicholas had no weapon. They would hack him into pieces.

But then a hand grabbed him. He wheeled around to face Jeremy. Jeremy smiled in wonderment. He had dismounted—and Martin, Pedro, and the boy called Will were with him. For one unforgettable second they looked upon one another with a surge of joy and triumph that they all felt. Then they clasped arms.

The five had come together.

And suddenly they were untouchable. Although the soldiers milled around them, it was as if they were inside a crystal jar. Swords flashed down uselessly. A forest of spears splintered and broke. Black shapes struggled in hopeless confusion. Nicholas, his arm clasped on one side by Jeremy and by Martin on the other, could feel the power flowing through him. All the energy in the world seemed to be contained inside him, and he was part of it. He couldn't have moved his hands if he had tried. He was aware only of four faces, all strangely alike, all set in silent concentration.

The circle had been formed.

And now something even stranger was happening. The circle had become a merry-go-round. They were spinning . . . but none of them were moving. It was the world that was spinning, Nicholas realized, outside the circle. Faster and faster it turned. The creatures had become a blur. There was a deafening crack. He looked up.

The sky had opened. A chasm had appeared, the fabric of the day peeling back to reveal the oblivion of eternal night. The sun's flames had exploded. The whole world was on fire. The wind howled around them, dashing up the sand, hurling it in the faces of their enemy, blinding them.

The King of the Old Ones screamed a second time. But now it was a howl of defeat and an incoherent vow of revenge.

It was over as quickly as it had begun.

The wind died down. The sand settled. The flow of power tapered away and ended. Suddenly exhausted, Nicholas felt his arms being released. He dropped them to his sides. For a last time, he turned his eyes upward.

The chasm was still there, a great gash in the heavens. Beneath it, what looked like a swarm of flies twisted up in a spiral. He watched as they were sucked into the void. There was a distant rumble of thunder and the sky rolled back, healing its self-inflicted wound. The Old Ones were gone. And at last a sun that Nicholas recognized shone high above, bright yellow and benevolent.

"It's over," Martin said. "The victory is ours."

"Nicholas . . ."

Jeremy stood facing him. And it was Jeremy: the same straw-colored hair, the same brown eyes. But Jeremy was still a prisoner in New York, far away in another world. And was he Nicholas? Pedro had told him that Nicholas had died the day before, had been carried to the plateau and buried.

"I don't understand," he said.

Martin stepped forward. He was smiling, but his face was touched by sadness. "There is no human answer," he said.

"We are not human. We never were. We were born apart . . . the five. We have come together here, now; and we will join together again one day so far in the future that we cannot number the years."

He turned to Jeremy.

"Nicholas is dead, Jeremy. He had to die. It was only because the Old Ones thought they had broken the circle that we were able to defeat them. Now, at last, they are locked out of the world. Today we have built a gate. One day it will have a name—the Devil's Door-bell."

"So the injection did kill me," Nicholas said.

Martin shook his head. "No. It would have killed an ordinary child, but you are not ordinary. It sent you back here. The Nicholas who died yesterday, the Nicholas we buried, he was another Nicholas. And it is another Jeremy who now needs your help.

"Don't you see? Time and space are nothing to us. It doesn't matter if we are in the present—now—or in the future. Pedro and Will and Jeremy and you and me. We are the five. We always will be."

A low moaning reached their ears. The victory had not been bloodless. The soldiers of the pentagram lay scattered across the plateau, some stretched out in the dust. Many had died and many more were wounded. Some were helping others to their feet, staggering together in the direction of the oasis. The women were running toward them, carrying bandages and water.

"What happens now?" Nicholas asked.

"You must go back into your own world," Martin said. "You still have your own battle to fight. You must save your brother. But we can help you."

He reached into his belt and pulled out a dagger, short and slender. The handle was white, with the blue pentagram set at the cross just above the silver blade.

"This belonged to Nicholas," Martin said. "The Nicholas we knew. Take it with you. It has been stained with the blood of the Old Ones and it has the power to kill their queen. But it is for you to find the courage to use it."

"But how do I get back?"

"We can send you there."

Nicholas slid the knife into his pocket. Then he laid a hand on Jeremy's shoulder. "I'm sorry, Jeremy," he said. "About Nicholas, I mean . . ."

Jeremy smiled although his eyes were filled with tears. "Don't be," he said. "I understand now. Nicholas will never die completely. Not while you're alive."

"It's time," Martin said.

The four boys closed in on Nicholas.

"Good luck," Pedro muttered.

"We'll meet again," Martin said.

Nicholas closed his eyes.

= SIXTEEN =

A Medical Impossibility

HE WAS BEING racked. His feet were a mile away from his knees and his head was slowly being pulled off his neck. He tried to speak, but his throat was dry and burning. His stomach had never been more empty. It was as if he had been scooped hollow. He was lying on his back, his hands resting loosely at his sides. A sheet and blanket had been drawn up to his chin. He was aware of the weight of them pressing down on him and the curve of the mattress beneath. He felt like the filling in a giant sandwich.

Nicholas opened his eyes, then screwed them shut again. Two huge suns were blazing in front of him. Cautiously, he opened them for a second time. The suns slid away, merged into one, and then dissolved into a 40-watt bulb in a gooseneck lamp. A figure loomed over him, a woman dressed in white. He had never seen her before.

"Drink this," she said.

A plastic cup touched his lips and he sipped. A trickle of ice cold orange juice ran over his tongue and down the back of his throat. He sipped again more greedily and choked.

"Not so quickly," the woman said.

He allowed her to feed him half a cup. After that he slept.

When he awoke later that evening, he was more aware of his surroundings. He was in a private room in a hospital. He could hear the names of doctors booming down the corridors, called out over the PA system, and there was a sharp antiseptic smell in the air. He lifted one hand and read his own name on a plastic bracelet attached to his wrist. A vase of flowers and a basket of fruit stood on a table beside his bed. The woman who had given him the orange juice—a young nurse—was still there, waiting for him to wake up. As soon as she saw that his eyes were open, she came over and took his pulse.

"How are you feeling?" she asked.

"Thirsty . . . and hungry," Nicholas said.

"That's good. I'll send for some supper."

"Thank you, Jill."

The nurse stopped and eyed him cautiously. She hadn't told him her name and she carried no mark of identification. So how . . . ? Shaking her head, she called on an inside phone and a few minutes later an orderly appeared, carrying a tray. Nicholas managed to drink his way through two glasses of fruit juice, but despite his appetite, he could only manage a little poached fish. His throat and stomach were still too sore.

"Where am I?" he asked.

"In a hospital in Brooklyn," the nurse told him.

"Where's that?"

"Just across the river from Manhattan."

"How long have I been here?"

"Thirty hours." The nurse took away the plate. "You were on a stomach pump yesterday, so you'll be feeling a little rough inside. You've got some nasty scratches on your stomach, and your pulse is rather high." She smiled. "The doctor says that you're a medical impossibility."

"What's that mean?"

"It means you should be dead."

The door opened and Linda bounded in, followed by a man carrying yet more fruit and flowers. It took Nicholas a few seconds to recognize him in his clean shirt and cords. It was the special agent, Bob Young.

"Nicholas . . ." Linda sat down on his bed, taking Nicholas's hand in her own. "God, I've been so worried about you. How are you?"

"I'm okay."

Bob Young stepped forward, brandishing the gifts. "I brought you these," he said. He gestured at the table. "But I guess Linda already beat me to it." He turned to the nurse and thrust the fruit and flowers into her arms. "Here you are, nurse. Take them home. But in return I'd like half an hour in private with the kid.''

The nurse scowled. ''Ten minutes,'' she said. ''And not a minute longer.'' She gave Nicholas one last thoughtful look, then left the room.

Nobody spoke.

Linda squeezed Nicholas's hand more tightly. ''What they did to you—'' She bit her lip. ''It makes me sick to think about it.''

''What exactly did they do to me?'' Nicholas asked.

''They only pumped you with enough heroin to kill a horse,'' Bob Young replied. He drew up a chair. ''Mind if I sit down? I'm probably not one of your favorite people right now. But I want to help.''

''The heroin . . .'' Nicholas muttered.

''It should have killed you,'' Bob said. ''I don't understand why it didn't. They dumped you in a back street in Harlem and that's where you were found . . . fortunately by a cop. He rushed you into Emergency. You were in a coma for twelve hours. Nobody thought you would pull through.''

Gently, Nicholas released his hand from Linda's grip. She had been holding it so tightly that her fingers had left white marks. He realized what she must have been through since his arrest and subsequent disappearance. In some ways it must have been even harder for her.

''Where did they take you?'' she asked. ''Mrs. Carnitt told me about some sort of prison on Roosevelt Island.''

''That's right.'' Briefly, Nicholas described what he had seen on the island: the two prison blocks, the printing works, the heroin factory. Neither Linda nor Bob spoke while he talked. Their faces were pale. That such a place could exist anywhere in the world was unlikely enough. That it did exist, and in the middle of New York, was beyond belief.

Nicholas finished. ''What happened to you after I'd gone?'' he asked.

Linda sighed. ''The call from the literary agent, that was a fake of course,'' she said. ''By the time I got back to the apartment, you'd gone.''

''Did you get my message?''

''No.'' She shook her head. ''They stole my message tape. So I went to see Mrs. Carnitt. I thought she might help. But while I was in her office, I guessed. She called you, didn't she? It was she you went to meet in Grand Central Station."

Nicholas nodded.

"I didn't know what to do after that," Linda went on. "Then, while I was walking home, Bob and one of his men picked me up. They scared the daylights out of me, I can tell you. For a moment I thought it was Mrs. Carnitt."

"That day we met at the World Trade Center," Bob broke in. "I didn't believe you. I'm sorry, Nick—believe me. But I figured there was enough in what you were saying to make it worth contacting my controller . . . Mr. Smith. That was his real name, by the way. I asked him to go to the Fulton Fish Market, just in case."

"So it was him . . ."

"That's right," Bob said. "They killed him. There was I, keeping tabs on a couple of junkies on the Lower East Side, while you three . . . I should have taken you more seriously. What happened was my fault."

He fell silent. Nicholas straightened up in his bed. He was still weak, but he could feel his strength returning with every second that passed. And he was different. He couldn't feel what it was, but he knew that something inside him had changed. It was as if part of him *had* died. In the past thirty hours he had lost something. And he knew that he would never be quite the same again.

"I suppose there's one thing we'll never know," Linda said.

"What's that?" Nicholas asked.

"Why the drug didn't kill you. I mean . . . there is no explanation."

"There might be," Nicholas said. "I'm not sure you'll believe it, but I'll tell you if you like."

"Go ahead," Bob said.

"All right. The heroin would have killed an ordinary kid but, well, I'm not ordinary. And it did something crazy to me. You say I was in a coma. In a way, I suppose I was. But at the same time"—Nicholas took a deep breath—"somehow the injection sent me back in time. Right back . . . to the beginning of time . . ."

He spoke, uninterrupted, for another five minutes. Either the bribe of fruit and flowers had worked, or the nurse had other matters to see to, but she didn't reappear. In a soft, emotionless voice, Nicholas spoke of Martin and Pedro, of the Shape-Changer and the great battle. He described the forming of the first circle and the banishment of the Old Ones.

"That was the trick," he explained. "The first Nicholas, the Nicholas who existed in that time, had died. So I was brought back to replace him. And when it was all over, they sent me back here, to finish what I'd started. I guess that must have been when I woke up."

There was another long silence.

That's some hallucination.

"It wasn't a hallucination, Mr. Young. . . ."

"Bob . . ."

"It wasn't a hallucination, Bob. It happened."

"All right!" Bob held up his hands. "You read my mind."

The words were spoken jokingly, but Nicholas didn't smile. "As a matter of fact, I did do just that," he said. "I always could. But before, it was difficult. I had to concentrate. Now I can do it"—he snapped his fingers—"like that."

"Now, just a minute!" Bob leaned forward. "I know I didn't believe you about the heroin, and I was wrong. But that was different. Heroin is a fact of life, and if I didn't have all the facts . . . well, I do now. But mind reading? Devils and black magic? That's nothing to do with the real world, Nick . . . unless it is all a hallucination. And, boy, did you have a hallucination! But forget it now. You're through it. It's over."

"You don't think I can read your thoughts?" Nicholas asked.

"I'm sorry. No."

"Then how do I know that you drove here in a blue convertible? Or that Mr. Smith's first name was Philip? Or that the nurse's name is Jill Green? How do I know that there are two men outside in the corridor guarding this room? One of them is called Baker and you don't like him. Tell me how I know that you and Linda had a hamburger before you came here tonight."

Bob's mouth fell open. Nicholas sank back into the pillow. He was tired again. He just wanted the whole thing to be over.

"It doesn't matter really what you think," he continued. "You know about Mrs. Carnitt now. You can raid the island, get the heroin, and find Jeremy. That's all that matters."

"It—it won't be as easy as that, Nick." All the confidence had gone out of Bob's voice.

"Why not?"

"There are laws, procedures. Mrs. Carnitt is still a powerful woman. Look, I believe you. I believe everything. But nobody else will, Nick. You can go and thought-read the President himself and it won't help. What I'm trying to say is, it'll take time. We have to get a search warrant. Maybe we're talking about a few days. Maybe a week."

"We don't have a week!" Nicholas exclaimed. "The drugs are moving. On Thanksgiving Day. And Jeremy doesn't have a week either. We have to find him."

"But we need a warrant."

"We don't have time."

Nicholas turned away. He wanted to sleep. Linda nodded at Bob and the two of them stood up. But as they moved toward the door, she turned back again. "I knew it wasn't a hallucination, Nick," she said. "I knew all along. There's something you ought to see."

Quickly, she walked across to a drawer and pulled it open.

"When they found you in Harlem, you were holding something. You were holding it so tightly, they couldn't get it out of your hands. I took it. It's here—and it may help."

When she turned around, she had something in her hands. Nicholas recognized it at once: the white hilt with the blue pentagram.

It was the dagger that Martin had given him.

= SEVENTEEN =

Covert Action

TO THE ASTONISHMENT of his nurses and the outrage of his doctor, Nicholas left the hospital the following morning. The doctor tried to forbid it, but after one quick word with Bob Young, he was forced to back down. The special agent had drawn on the resources of the FBI both to protect Nicholas while he was in the hospital and to ease his way out. No word of his activities had reached the press. And his name had been erased from the police computer. The inquiry into the murder of Don White was officially closed.

Things were happening, Nicholas knew. But sitting once again in Linda's apartment, he wondered if they were happening quickly enough. As Bob had explained, it was only his word against Mrs. Carnitt's, and what sort of contest was that? A pillar of New York society against one dispossessed boy. A major benefactress of countless charities against one obvious crank. Bob had worked through the night, making calls, collecting dossiers, and chasing information. But there still wasn't enough real evidence. Not enough to raid the island. Not enough to stop the heroin leaving it.

Bob got back to the apartment in the late afternoon, red-eyed and unshaven. Linda got him a beer from the refrigerator and he sat down heavily, stretching out his legs.

"Read my mind yet, Nick?" he asked as he opened the beer.

"I don't need to," Nicholas said.

"You're right there." He shook his head. "It's hopeless. Nobody believes me because nobody wants to believe me. Mrs. Carnitt has too many powerful friends. If she goes, quite a few important people will go with her."

"Why?" Linda asked.

Bob drained the can of beer. "Suppose you're a politician," he said. "Or the head of a major corporation. You've managed to raise a million dollars and you've given it to the Golden Cup. Then someone comes along and tells you that the money was used to buy heroin. Well, your own future's not going to look too bright, is it?"

"So what can we do?" Nicholas sighed. "By tomorrow it'll be too late."

Bob had been carrying a leather case when he came in. Now he set it on his knees and unlocked it.

"We can take covert action," he said.

"Covert?" Nicholas repeated.

"Unauthorized, undercover, probably illegal . . ." He took out two sheets of paper and unfolded them. "I want to go to the island myself, tonight."

"How?" Linda asked.

"That's a good question. The trouble is, the southern tip of Roosevelt Island is run as a maximum-security prison. That means watchtowers and armed guards . . . and it's all perfectly legit." He spread the sheets of paper out on the carpet. The top one was a map of the island with all the buildings marked. "This is a map of the compound based on records and on what Nick told me. Now, I can't get across on the cable car. Everyone traveling to the prison is checked, and anyway, I'd still have to get through the main gate."

"What about a boat?" Linda suggested.

"No go. Look at the position of the watchtowers. All three sides are covered. There's a full moon tonight, but even without it they'd see me before I got anywhere near."

"What's this?" Nicholas asked, pointing to a small square marked "53rd Street Exit."

"That, my friend, is the way in," Bob replied. He slid the other sheet across. "This is a map of the New York subway system," he went on. "As you can see, nearly all the lines run vertically, north to south. But this line here"—he tapped the paper—"runs horizontally, out to Queens. It passes right underneath the island, and there's an emergency exit that comes out in the prison compound itself."

"It'll be locked," Linda said.

"It is locked," Bob agreed. "But from underneath. I have the key. And I've cleared it with the MTA—that's the Metropolitan Transportation Authority. Tonight I'm taking the subway from Fifty-third Street. But I'm going by foot."

There was a pause. Nicholas looked from one map to the other. "What will you do when you get there?" he asked.

"I'll try to find Jeremy, for a start," Bob said. "I'll be in radio contact with my department, and if I get into trouble, I'll be able to call for backup." He smiled grimly. "It breaks all the rules, but if anyone takes a shot at me, I can have half the FBI in there in five minutes and take the consequences tomorrow."

"You want them to shoot at you," Linda said.

Bob shrugged. "Of course. It's the only way I can get my men in." He picked up the maps and folded them again.

"When are you going?" Nicholas asked.

"I'll leave here at midnight."

"I'm coming too."

"Now, wait a minute." Bob held up his hands. "There's no way . . ."

"I'm going with you," Nicholas insisted. "If Jeremy is still on the island, you won't know where to look. And once your men bust in, they'll kill him. I can find him. If he's there, I'll know."

"That may be true, but—"

"And there's another thing," Nicholas broke in.

"Yeah?"

"My power, Bob. I don't like it and I don't want it, but in the last few days it's grown. Right now I feel like a sort of battery. I should be dead, but I'm stronger that I've ever been. I can help you. I have to help you."

Bob thought for a moment. Then he nodded. "All right," he said. "Then that makes it two of us."

"Three," Linda said.

"Three?" Bob looked at Linda in amazement. "What do you mean?"

"I'm coming too."

"But . . . why?"

Linda glanced at Nicholas. "Because he's my friend."

"I can't argue with that," Nicholas said.

"And I can't argue with either of you." Bob stood up tiredly. "I'm going to get some sleep," he said. "If I were you, I'd do the same. We leave at midnight."

The train was a strange, primeval monster, roaring through the tunnel in a storm of bright light and stale air. Pressed against the tunnel wall, Nicholas was aware only of the grinding metal wheels and a streak of graffiti, with the windows high above. And then it had turned a corner, the rumble dying behind it, and they were left alone in the great stretch of darkness, lit only by the dim and dusty light bulbs set at intervals in the ceiling.

"All right. Let's move," Bob said. He swung a powerful flashlight around on Linda and Nicholas. Although they were far underground somewhere underneath the East River, he spoke in a whisper. "And watch that third rail."

"The third rail," Linda muttered. "The third rail . . ." She had said little else since Bob had warned her that if she so much as sneezed on it, the electricity would fry her to a frazzle.

There are seven hundred miles of subway track in and around New York. Bob, Nicholas, and Linda were making their way along one of the longest stretches, stepping over murky puddles and scattered heaps of rubbish. Nicholas stepped on an old McDonald's carton and felt it crumple under his foot. In the cavernous silence the sound seemed ridiculously loud. Both Linda and Bob snapped around accusingly. How had it gotten there? Nicholas wondered. Who would want to eat a hamburger down here?

They reached an iron ladder welded against one wall and continuing up through the ceiling in a cylindrical tube. Bob consulted his map, then flicked off the flashlight.

"This is it," he said. "I'll go first, then Nicholas. But you don't come out until I give the word. Okay?"

He climbed the ladder and disappeared into the tunnel. Hanging a few rungs below him, Nicholas could see the moonlight stabbing through three holes in the exit. This was a circular lid, like a manhole cover, fastened with two bolts and a heavy padlock. Bob drew back the bolts and unlocked the lid with the key he had been given. Gently, he raised it, peered through the crack, then climbed out.

A few seconds passed. Then came a whispered command. Nicholas followed him out, with Linda close behind, and a moment later the three of them were crouching together in the cold night air. For some reason it was much colder above ground than it had been below. Even the light from the moon was cold and the wind gusting across the water of the East River had the touch of ice.

There was nobody in sight, but as they took their bearings, a beam from one of the watchtowers rippled across the ground, passing only inches from them. The subway exit was sheltered by a low wall and they hugged the bricks, not daring to move. The light curved away, momentarily broken by the corner of the building that housed the specials, but still the moon shone. Inwardly, Nicholas cursed it. Why did this night of all nights have to be cloudless?

"Nick!" Bob whispered. Nicholas felt his hand on his shoulder. "Is he here?"

Nicholas closed his eyes, sending his thoughts out across the island. Even Mrs. Carnitt had told him that his brother had left the island, and for once she had been speaking the truth. But he was aware of something. Somebody on the island knew that he was there. He had often thought of himself as a transmitter, and now, whatever energy he was sending out was being received. But not by Jeremy.

He shook his head.

"Okay. Where's the main block?"

Nicholas pointed across the parking lot. There were only about half a dozen cars parked there beneath the castlelike battlements of Block A. No lights shone behind the prison windows, but the moon glinted off the iron bars. They had come up behind the guards' quarters and that, too, was dark and silent. The island was asleep, but it had left an eye open. He could see a figure moving in the watchtower to his left and the beam never paused in its slow track across the lawns.

"The heroin?" Bob whispered.

"In the basement. Mr. Banes took me through an entrance around the side."

"Right. You two stay here."

There was a small box attached to Bob's belt; a radio connecting him with his backup. He had left the map and the flashlight at the foot of the ladder. In his right hand he held a gun. He smiled briefly at Nicholas and Linda, then, half-crouching, sprinted across the parking lot, his sneakers making no sound on the tarmac.

"What do we do now?" Linda whispered.

"We wait," Nicholas replied.

"And now?"

Two guards had appeared, walking down the path toward them, their feet crunching on the gravel. Scraping their backs against the bricks, Nicholas and Linda pulled themselves along the wall and out of sight. But as they turned the corner, Linda's foot caught a loose stone and it rolled forward. The guards stopped. There was a click as they released the safety catches on their automatic rifles. Slowly, confidently, they continued on, heading straight for the subway exit, their guns probing through the darkness.

Linda swore under her breath. Nicholas pulled Martin's dagger out of his belt.

Then the alarms sounded.

The noise was deafening. Sirens exploded throughout the island: on the corners of the buildings, in the trees, on pillars set waist-high along the paths. Lights flashed on behind the windows of the guards' quarters as half-dressed men ran out in the open, spilling into the night. The spotlights became frantic, snaking back and forth across the ground. There was a burst of gunfire from the side of Block A, the direction that Bob Young had taken.

But there was no time to worry about Bob. The two guards had seen them. They stopped a few paces away, their guns leveled. Neither of them spoke. They clearly didn't mean to ask any questions. There were intruders on the island. Intruders had to die. That was all. And as if there were any chance of their missing even at such close range, the spotlight suddenly caught them in its dazzling grip, pinning them against the wall. Nicholas and Linda drew themselves up, blinking. The two guards took aim.

But then the rifles had been torn out of their hands, spinning away into the night. It was as if the guards had had enough, had thrown them away, except that their arms hadn't moved. The guns had been jerked from them, seized by an invisible hand. The guards hesitated, staring at Nicholas. Linda was looking at him too. But he hadn't done it. . . .

And then the guards followed their guns, rose off their feet, and catapulted through the air, their arms and legs spinning. They traveled—flew—perhaps a hundred yards, finally crashing into the concrete on the far side of the parking lot, where they lay still.

A tall dark-haired boy about seventeen years old stood on the lawn facing them. His eyes had followed the two guards as they hurtled past him, but now he turned back as if awaiting orders. More children appeared behind him, all dressed in uniform blue denim with numbers stenciled in black ink on their shirts. The boy's number was 253.

For a long minute they stood without speaking, the sirens still blasting all around them. Something was flashing in the darkness. Nicholas looked up. The machine-gun in the watchtower was firing at them. It was incredible. He could see the white flame spitting out of the muzzle. But not a single bullet was reaching them. The children seem unconcerned, untouched by the hail of bullets. Only Linda drew close to him, her eyes filled with fear and incomprehension.

But Nicholas understood. When he had first heard the alarms, he had thought that Bob had been captured and that it was his discovery that had triggered them off. But it hadn't happened that way. It was something else, something quite extraordinary.

He had been right. His power had grown—but more even than he had supposed. He had become a sort of beacon. There were seventy or more specials on the island, children with powers similar to his own. But their powers had been dormant, underdeveloped. They were capable of flashes, uncontrolled bursts of clairvoyance, mind reading, or whatever. But once he had arrived on the island, all that had changed.

Now they were an army. He had lent them his strength, drawn out their power and multiplied it a hundredfold. He had found them when he had sent out his thoughts in a last attempt to reach Jeremy. Or they had found him. At that moment their power had awakened. They had broken out of their cells. That was what had set off the alarms. And now they were waiting for him to command them.

"What's your name?" he asked the dark-haired boy. His words were inaudible in the general din, but still the boy heard him.

"Paul," he said. "I was here when they brought in your brother."

"But Jeremy's gone."

"Yes."

Nicholas looked around tiredly. It had seemed as if time were suspended on the island, but now more guards came running toward them. The noise of the sirens was louder than ever.

"Finish it," he said.

Another boy with hair so fair that it was almost white glanced up at the watchtower, where the machine-gun was still crackling uselessly. That was all he did. But a second later the entire structure exploded in a ball of flame that threw crimson shadows from one end of the island to the other. At the same time, the group of children broke up, moving slowly toward the various buildings. Three guards about fifty yards away lifted automatic rifles. Another child—a girl this time—turned toward them. The three men died on their feet.

"Come on," Nicholas said.

"Where are we going?" Linda asked.

"We'd better find Bob."

They crossed the lawn as the island disintegrated about them. One at a time, the windows of the guards' quarters were breaking, whirling glass cutting through the night. Cables tore themselves out of the ground. The very trees erupted. A wave of energy so intense that they could almost see it shimmered across the island, destroying everything in its path.

Nicholas and Linda reached Gallows Way and hurried forward toward Block A. It was quieter and darker here on the side of the island that faced away from Manhattan. Linda was about ten paces behind Nicholas, her ears ringing from the noise of the sirens, her head throbbing. She glanced back at the mayhem they had left behind them. Block B was on fire. The legs of the last watchtower had bent and split. High above, a guard was thrashing at the air as the whole thing tilted, then collapsed. She turned back.

"Nicholas!" she shouted.

A figure had stepped out of the shadows at the edge of the guards' quarters, pouncing on Nicholas from behind. It was a figure dressed in a dark suit, tall and thin, with perfectly round glasses. Linda had never seen him before, but she recognized him at once: Mr. Banes. Nicholas hardly had time to react. With the sirens still at full blast, he hadn't heard Linda's warning. Mr. Banes swung a loop of wire weighted at one end in a single, practiced movement. It twisted around Nicholas's neck, jerking him back off his feet. As Linda ran forward, Mr. Banes began to pull. The wire bit into Nicholas's flesh.

The garotte could have killed him in seconds, but at the last moment Nicholas had managed to get three fingers between the wire and his throat. Even so, he was being strangled slowly. Desperately, he clawed at the wire, trying to keep it from his wind pipe. Mr. Banes pulled with all his strength, kneeling beside Nicholas as he sank to his knees, his thin lips stretched in an ugly smile.

Linda hurled herself at Mr. Banes, battering the back of his head with her clenched fists. The man barely seemed to feel her. She wrenched at his hair and shuddered in disgust as a clump of lifeless gray strands came away in her hand. There were only seconds left. Nicholas was white, his eyes bulging. And still Mr. Banes pulled, his face set in grim concentration.

The hearing aid . . . A plan formed in Linda's mind and she snatched it, tearing it away from behind Mr. Banes's ear. Now she was holding it in her hand, a black cable like a telephone wire curling into the ear itself. The volume control was turned down to its lowest level. With trembling fingers Linda turned it back to full. There was a concrete pillar set beside the road, a siren blaring at them from the top. Cradling the hearing aid in her palm, she stretched the wire as far as it would go and pressed it against the siren.

The screech of the siren, amplified twenty times, pulsed down the wire and into Mr. Banes's brain. It was a noise beyond human endurance. Nicholas felt the wire loosen around his neck. He saw Mr. Banes's mouth open in a silent, agonized scream. The man's skin seemed to stretch like elastic.

Then his eyes, behind the circular glasses, exploded. Mr. Banes crumpled to one side, his legs and arms twitching even after death. A moment later the sirens fell silent. Somewhere on the island a circuit had fused.

Shaking all over, Linda knelt beside Nicholas. "Nick . . . are you okay?" she cried.

Nicholas rubbed his throat, painfully sucking at the air. He looked at the body of Mr. Banes lying spread out on the gravel. "Wow," he said. He swallowed. "That was a bit of an eye-opener."

With the alarms still, new sounds ruled the island. The crackle of flames and the splintering of wood. Gunfire. The shouts of the guards as they were destroyed by a power they did not understand and which they could no longer control. Linda heard someone running down the path toward them. She didn't move, too exhausted to fight anymore.

It was Bob Young.

"What are you doing here?" he demanded. "What the hell's going on?" Then he noticed the welt on Nicholas's throat. "Are you all right, kid?" he asked more gently.

"Sure." Nicholas stood up. "Did you find the heroin?"

Bob nodded. "Yes. Then they found me. What's happening?"

"The island's closing down," Nicholas said.

And it was. The flames had spread to Block A, and the ordinary prisoners were free, streaming through the main gate and out to the cable car station. At the far end of the island there was a deep rumbling, and Linda was astonished to see white light streaming upward as if from the ground itself. The road trembled beneath her feet.

She followed Bob and Nicholas down Gallows Way, remembering from the map that it led to the building know as the Treatment Center. But when she reached the bottom, the Treatment Center was gone. All the children from Block B were grouped around a wide crater. Smoke billowed upward. A brilliant light pulsated far below. Not a brick, not a stick of wood remained. The Treatment Center had been obliterated forever.

There was a whirling sound in the air. A helicopter had appeared, hovering above the flames. For a moment it rocked over the island. Then it descended, its great blades spinning in a vortex of dirt and dust. Bob's reinforcements had arrived.

Nicholas walked away.

"Where are you going now?" Linda called out.

Nicholas turned around, silhouetted against the flames. "To get Jeremy," he said.

= EIGHTEEN =

Jeremy and Nicholas

THANKSGIVING DAY IN New York City. The fourth Thursday in November.

It had begun as it always began, with a procession that wound its way down Broadway to the huge Macy's department store. Despite the cold, thousands of people jostled for position on the sidewalks while millions more watched it on television. They were waving flags and cheering. Music and laughter filled the air.

The procession seemed to go on forever. There were multicolored floats trundling slowly past, cowboys riding horses and clowns on papier-mâché caterpillars, bands and dancers. And as ever, there were the balloons, filled with helium and enormous, each one held down by up to twenty people at the ends of thick cables. Snoopy, Superman, Kermit, Donald Duck . . . one after another they sailed past, bobbing against the glittering skyscrapers.

Fifth Avenue was deserted as Nicholas walked down from Central Park. It was as if the entire population of the city had been magically spirited away.

He had left Linda and Bob on the island, looking after the special children who remained. There was also the heroin to be dealt with. Thousands of crates had been found in a network of cellars underneath Block A. Neatly packed in plastic bags and hidden in hollowed-out Bibles, the heroin had been ready for its deadly journey all over the nation. Bob had tested a sample and found it to be ten percent pure. Had it ever reached the streets of America, the consequences would have been unimaginable.

A few cars raced past, taking advantage of the traffic-free avenue. A handful of pedestrians hurried along the sidewalk, making for Broadway and the parade. The sky was clear and bright, with just a few powdery clouds. Nicholas walked on at a steady pace. He knew now where he was going. He knew where to find Jeremy.

The Silver Citadel.

Its shape had reminded him of something the moment he saw it, but it was only now that he could make the connection. Narrowest at the bottom, with a vast cylinder leading up to a glittering needle . . . Evelyn Carnitt had designed it, of course. Only she could have had that chilling sense of humor.

She had built it to resemble a colossal hypodermic syringe.

And there it was, still and silent. The building was empty now, the shops and restaurants closed. Nicholas paused on the opposite side of the avenue. Steam was rising out of a manhole in the middle of the road, curling around the entrance. The traffic lights changed. DONT WALK . . . DONT WALK . . . they flashed in red. A warning?

Nicholas crossed the street. The doors of the Citadel slid open long before he could have activated the infra-red beam.

He was expected.

For a moment he wanted to turn and run while he still could. But he forced himself forward. Only when he had reached the doors themselves did he pause for a second time. It seemed very dark inside. Nothing moved. The trees in the inner courtyard were strangely colorless. The fountains were still. Clenching his fists, Nicholas stepped off the sidewalk and into the Citadel, out of the sunlight and into darkness. With a soft hiss the door slid shut behind him.

He walked down the passage past the piano and crossed the courtyard, trying not to look at the glass panels on the walls. It was as if they had become windows. Something was moving behind them, something dark and evil. He was being watched. Tiny pinpricks of light glowed in the twisting clouds. Something very much like a hand reached out, the webbed fingers pressing against the fragile barrier. It was cold in the Citadel, too cold. He felt as if he had stepped into a giant refrigerator.

He stopped in the center of the courtyard. Something had caught his eye. He raised his head. At first he thought it was a net stretched across the opening between the escalators. A misshapen bundle was caught up in the middle of it, one limb hanging down. Then, with a shudder, he realized what he was looking at. The net was a huge spider's web. The bundle was Albert Worm. He was a tangle of unmoving muscles, one arm dangling beneath the mess that was his body. So Mrs. Carnitt had killed him. Why? Because his usefulness had come to an end—or because he had made one mistake too many?

There was a rattle and an elevator door opened, light spilling out. Nicholas was walking into a trap. He knew it, but he had no choice. The elevator might take him to the seventieth floor, then drop like a stone, smashing him on impact. It might not move at all, instead bursting into flames and roasting him within its four walls. He went in and the doors closed. Evelyn Carnitt was waiting for him. She wanted to see him. Then, perhaps, she would kill him.

The elevator sped upward of its own accord. Once again the dark mirrors were transparent and Nicholas could see through them, out onto an incredible world. It was a world similar to the one he had visited in his first dream, the night he had met Martin. He was on the other side of the dark sea, and now he could make out the ghostly shapes of the Old Ones, gathered on the shore, their eyes following him as he soared up above them. It was as if he were traveling in a rocket out of hell, and he was grateful when the elevator slowed down and stopped, the doors sliding open to release him.

He stepped out into a short corridor leading to a set of double doors. White mist that had somehow followed him in from the street rippled out of the elevator behind him, its tentacles creeping cold around his ankles. There was a black statue—a panther—on each side of the doors. At least they had looked like statues. But as he approached, they rose on their haunches, growling softly. A clawed foot snatched at the air. A head turned, teeth snapping at him. The doors opened inward. Nicholas walked past and went in.

Evelyn Carnitt was standing in front of a window that looked like a movie screen, framing a vast panorama of New

York. It had been daylight, early morning, when Nicholas went in. But seen through the curving glass, the city was shrouded in night. She, too, was dressed in black, the dull gold of her jewelry her only color. She made no movement as Nicholas stood in front of her, but her lips twisted into a cruel smile.

"Nicholas Helsey," she hissed in a voice that was more animal than human. "You came, as I knew you would."

Nicholas said nothing, rooted to the spot by her unforgiving eyes.

"I thought I had killed you," she went on. "But it seems to be more difficult than I had thought to kill one of the five. You have managed to destroy a major operation. You have set back the cause of the Old Ones by perhaps a year. But that is all you have done, boy. A delay, not a defeat."

"I've come for Jeremy," Nicholas said.

"Jeremy!" She almost sang the word in a shrill mockery. "Jeremy has been waiting for you. I promised him you would come. And he is here. Turn around, boy. Turn around and see for yourself the power of the Old Ones."

Somebody moved out of the shadows at the corner of the room. Nicholas looked around.

It was Jeremy.

Or was it? His appearance had changed. His hair had been cut short and he had lost weight. Like Evelyn Carnitt, he was dressed in black: black trousers and a black silk shirt fastened at the neck. He was looking at Nicholas with a hatred that was almost inhuman. His lips were stretched in a grimace. His eyes were pitiless.

"Jeremy . . ." Nicholas whispered.

"You left me." Somehow it wasn't his brother's voice. But it was Jeremy who had spoken. "You betrayed me."

"No!"

It was useless arguing. His brother—the creature that his brother had become—wouldn't listen. Nicholas reached for his belt. He turned back to face Evelyn Carnitt again, but now he was holding the dagger with its white hilt and blue pentagram. For a split-second she faltered and Jeremy hesitated, her hold over him weakened.

"You went back . . ." she whispered. And then she knew how the five had first defeated the Old Ones. It had been a trick . . . and all the more galling because it had been she who had made it possible.

With a hiss of anger she raised an arm. It was as if an invisible whip had lashed into Nicholas's hand. He cried out. The dagger spun away from him and slid across the carpet, coming to rest a few inches from where Jeremy stood. Nicholas cradled his hand. He wondered if his fingers were broken.

Jeremy picked up the dagger.

"Do you really think you can kill me?" Mrs. Carnitt cried. "Alone, you are an insect to be crushed underfoot. You have been an irritation, boy. Worm should have killed you when he had the chance . . . and he has paid the price. Now it is your turn. You came in search of your brother and you have found him. But now he serves me. He will always serve me. All you have found is your death."

Jeremy moved forward one step at a time, the dagger gripped in his hand. He was like an automaton; mindless, emotionless. Nicholas wanted to run, but he couldn't move.

"Jeremy!" he shouted. "You can fight her. Listen to me!"

His brother showed no more than a flicker of annoyance. Still he came, the dagger raised, his face pale and deadly.

"Jeremy!"

Words couldn't reach him. But thoughts might.

"Jeremy!" He pushed harder than he ever had before. *"It's Nicholas. I'm your brother."*

Jeremy looked at Evelyn Carnitt.

"Kill him!" she screeched.

Nicholas pushed again. And suddenly he was inside his brother's head. Their two minds had fused into one, and he was sharing all the pain that Jeremy had suffered.

He was in the Treatment Center. He could feel the leather straps holding down his wrists. Mr. Banes was leaning over him, his own eyes—his brother's eyes—reflected in the circular glasses. A light was pulsing on and off, the flash burning yellow on his retinas. A terrible screaming sound filled his ears. He saw Mr. Banes reach for a switch and convulsed as a burst of electricity shuddered through him. Black wires like snakes shot through the air, sinking their fangs into his head.

"Nicholas betrayed you . . . Nicholas hated you."

He heard the soft, persuasive words.

"No, Jeremy. I searched for you. They were lying."

Another agonizing burst of electricity. On the far edge of his vision a green dot leaped across a television screen, monitoring his heart—his brother's heart. And there was Evelyn Carnitt, whispering soundlessly, the glowing end of her cigarette looming toward him.

More pain. The room spiraled away, disappearing down an endless tunnel. And now he was back outside the Comedy Theatre. He could see himself on the wall, the wind blowing in his hair, pointing down, laughing. He could see himself as Jeremy had been made to see him.

"It's not true, Jeremy. It didn't happen that way. You saved me."

He pushed and the image shattered. The wall, the theater, the men who had come for them . . . the entire picture exploded, spinning away in a thousand fragments, a moving jigsaw that Nicholas had destroyed.

And then, at last, a moment of silence. The two brothers were together in their dressing room, minutes before their flight. Jeremy was standing beside the door. Nicholas, the weaker of the two—for so he had been then—was staring at him, afraid.

"Whatever happens," Jeremy was saying, "I'm your brother, Nick. I always will be."

"Do you remember, Jeremy? You are. You still are. It doesn't matter what they've done to you."

Jeremy had stopped. Evelyn Carnitt took a step forward, her eyes blazing, her hands hooked above her head.

"Kill him!" she commanded. "Do it now!"

Jeremy threw the dagger. It made one complete revolution in the air, then buried itself in Evelyn Carnitt's throat. She opened her mouth to scream. Blood gushed over her lip. At the same moment, the skin seemed to peel away from her face. Nicholas saw her skull, the grinning teeth, the dark caverns of her eye sockets. Maggots dripped out of her hair. Black ooze poured out of her ears and nose. She took one step back, tripped, and fell. Then, as if carried by some supernatural force, her shoulders hit the huge window. The glass disintegrated all around her and at last she was gone, plunging backward into the night.

Jeremy and Nicholas stood facing each other.

"Jeremy . . ." Nicholas muttered.

"Nick . . ."

"I . . ."

They moved together. The ground shook.

The Citadel had been built, impossibly, in one year. And now that its creator had gone, it could no longer exist. The ceiling of the penthouse buckled. The rest of the window collapsed, the jagged edges splintering on the carpet. Somewhere far below there was a muffled explosion. Daylight streamed in through one wall as the bricks separated, a wide crack zigzagging its way across.

"Come on!" Nicholas shouted.

There was no time to argue. The two brothers ran to the door, then out into the corridor. It was only when he saw them that Nicholas remembered the panthers. They were there, waiting for them, about to pounce. But even as they watched they turned back into statues, cracked, and crumbled. At the far end of the corridor a whole wall slid away, cables and steel girders trailing in the air. Nicholas ran for the elevator, pulling himself back at the last second. The door was open, but the elevator wasn't there. Shredded wires and sparking fuses told their own story.

"The stairs!"

He pulled open a door beside the elevator and waited as Jeremy passed him. Behind him, part of the corridor erupted upward, the carpet tearing, the floorboards snapping. The whole building was trembling now as if seized by an earthquake.

Down they ran. Down, down, down . . . There were ninety-two floors between them and street level and the forces of destruction were only inches behind them. They would no sooner reach the bottom of one flight of stairs than it would shatter behind them, the concrete smashing, the iron banisters twisting themselves into knots. Down they ran. Once Jeremy tripped and Nicholas had to pull him back even as the wall collapsed, an iron girder battering through the plaster just in front of his head. He was dizzy now. How many times had he twisted around and around, following the staircase down? And the whole building was swaying, like a ship about to capsize in a storm. Smoke was thick in the air, seeping into the stairwell. The Citadel was burning.

But then, somehow, they reached the bottom. Jeremy stopped to rest, but Nicholas caught hold of his arm, dragging him across the courtyard and out past the piano. Worm had disappeared. The fountains were dry. One escalator had peeled upward, the metal steps spread in a crazy concertina across the shattered marble. Half-carrying his brother, Nicholas made for the door. The infra-red mechanism was broken. The door remained shut. But as he approached, the glass exploded outward and at last they were in the street, out in the daylight, running for the shelter of Central Park.

Behind them, in the far distance, Fifth Avenue was filled with the whoop of sirens as police cars rushed toward the scene.

The Silver Citadel snapped in half. For one last time, the great needle tore at the sky. The top half rammed into the jagged remains of the base. Then the whole thing crumbled in on itself, disappearing in a cloud of dust and flame.

= NINETEEN =

J.F.K.

"THIS IS THE last call for passengers on Flight VA five nine zero for Lima. Will passengers please proceed directly to Gate Forty-one where the flight to Lima is now boarding."

It was two weeks later, Nicholas picked up his hand luggage and walked through the glass doors that led into Kennedy Airport. It was a cold evening. Winter was drawing in. The plane was a short distance away, the rays of the dying sun reflected in the dull silver of its wings.

"Glad to be going, Nick?" Bob Young asked.

Nicholas nodded. "Yes."

"I wish I were coming with you. But you've left a hornet's nest behind you. First you've got a major charity that's actually peddling heroin. Then it turns out they're using a state prison as their base. And to cap it all, you've got one of New York's most famous landmarks reduced to a pile of dust! It's just a miracle that nobody was killed. If it had been any other day . . ." His voice trailed off. "I just want you to understand, Nick. I do want to go with you."

Nicholas smiled. "I do understand, Bob."

They walked on a little farther. The other passengers were already seated. The plane was waiting for them.

"Your brother . . ." Bob muttered.

Nicholas looked back. Jeremy was a short way behind, talking to Linda, who was struggling under the weight of enough hand luggage for the three of them, and more besides. "He's all right now," he said.

It was true. In just two short weeks Jeremy had become very much his old self. Linda had been looking after him, stuffing him with sausages, hamburgers, french fries, milk shakes—and just about anything else she could tempt him with.

Jeremy had put on a little weight. He was laughing again. And he was sleeping more easily. But even so, the nightmares still came and in moments of silence a pained, haunted look would creep back into his eyes.

"He's all right," Nicholas repeated.

And inwardly he swore that Jeremy would be all right. Martin was waiting for them in Peru. A few days before they had spoken on the phone. Nicholas had been strangely excited to hear his voice. So much had happened to him since his arrival in New York that he found it difficult to believe that Martin could actually exist in the real world.

But he was there and Pedro was with him . . . a boy gifted with the power of healing. Pedro would take care of Jeremy. The last memories of the island would be banished.

They reached the steps that led into the waiting jumbo jet. Nicholas took one last look at New York, the familiar landmarks standing out in the distance beyond the clutter of the airport. The sky overhead was clear, but even as he looked it seemed that the clouds were rolling back, the darkness gathering.

He shivered. The body of Evelyn Carnitt still hadn't been found.

Jeremy and Linda joined him, and the two boys shook hands with Bob.

"I'll see you again," Bob promised. "As soon as everything's straightened out here I'll follow you. Just look after yourselves until I get there." He kissed Linda and turned away.

Ten minutes later the plane took off, climbing swiftly into the sky. The no smoking sign blinked out and a stewardess appeared, pushing a beverage cart. Nicholas was sitting next to Jeremy, who had taken the window seat. He looked across the aisle and was astonished to see Linda removing a portable typewriter from one of her bags.

"What on earth are you doing?" he asked.

"My novel . . ." Linda explained. "It's eight hours to Lima and there's no time like the present."

"Another thriller?" Nicholas said.

"That's right. I thought I'd call it *A Deadly Day in November*."

The plane arced to the left, circling over New York, then turned south on its journey to Peru.